Super Vows

a novel by

Kevin Kelton

To Stephanie,

Happy reading!

Regards,

Kevin Kelton

Published: January 5, 2022

Words: 46,527

Language: English

ISBN: 9798796513897

DEDICATION

For Max and Elliot.

May they never have to live in a world like the one

you're about to enter.

Chapter 1

'*G*uess who's banging Myra.'

'Trouble in paradise for Chase and Dreyer.'

'Something's come between Derek and Ian. With the initials MD.'

At first, Ken Feldman didn't believe the rumors were real. Coming to him anonymously, in emails filled with grainy snapshots, they looked as questionable as most of the "tips" that came to his inbox. The tabloid business brings out the fruitcakes, along with gaggles of semi-crazy people who consider this actor or that rock star their mortal enemy. As if the actor or rocker in question even knows the other person is alive.

But when you're on the celebrity gossip desk at *The American Peephole*, you are the lucky recipient of every bit of sleaze or scandal that the human mind can imagine. U.S. senators involved in voodoo sex cults? Happens every day. Russian cosmonauts harvesting cloned Stalin brains in space? Makes complete sense.

And the gossip that comes in about

Hollywood megastars like super-couple Derek Chase and Myra Dreyer makes all that sound tame. Ken learned that in his first year on a news desk. But the gossip desk is a whole different animal. The things people claim to know about the private lives of celebrities, well, when you filter out the twenty per cent that is patently absurd, the rest of it is all relatively believable. Why wouldn't that male movie star put the moves on his happily married, formerly bulimic, recently detoxed co-star? And why wouldn't she succumb to his heralded sexual charms during a five month location shoot in Thailand? If you can't drink or snort or shoot, you might as well screw.

And if there was a shred of validity to the rumor – the most tenuous of evidence that it may be true – it was Ken Feldman's job to memorialize it in eight hundred shocking words. With pictures. No matter how good or solid the story was, at *The American Peephole* there was only one unshakable, non-debatable, omnipresent golden rule: no photo, no article. You could break Harry and Meghan expecting…hell, you could break the the death of Kobe Bryant. But unless you had a fresh photo of the happy couple or Kobe in a helicopter, your piece won't make it to print.

But that was never a problem on the gossip desk. Any two celebrities who you could conjure a rumor about had been photographed together at one point or another. All Ken had to do was string together a loose set of what passed for facts, add a few unattributed quotes and presto! – he had his eight hundred words and $800 for the week. It wasn't the kind of lofty income he'd envisioned when he graduated with a dual degree in Journalism and Psychology from Syracuse. But it was sure better than chasing down fatal car crash stories for *The Boston Advisor,* a pseudo-intellectual daily that catered to New England's so-called "serious news market."

Ken had written maybe a thousand of those crash articles in his two years at *The Advisor*, replete with every name, age, internal injury and alcohol level, but never, *never* with the make or model of the car that tipped and rolled seventeen times. Heaven forbid an auto manufacturer might file a law suit. Real newspapers hate lawsuits. Especially from giant corporations with their own legal departments and infinitely deep pockets.

Ken had tried to fight that rule of print journalism. When he had them, he would point to the photos of the burnt-out SUV shell and argue to his editors that any reader who knew anything about cars would be able to discern the make and model. To which his editors always argued, "Then why put it in print?" But Ken knew that most of the time the severity of the wreckage made the death vehicle indistinguishable from any other similar car. Ken wanted his readers to know that the "family car" they take their kids to school in has all the stability of a giraffe on roller blades. He always tried to sneak in a veiled reference to a popular SUV that had rolled out of a turn or a minivan that disintegrated upon impact. The editors always caught him. It became a game to them. An amusing aspect of the job.

"Nice try, Feld. You gonna fix it or should I?'

"What're you talking about?" Ken always said it with his best, wide-eyed bewilderment. Which wasn't very good.

"Lacerations caused by impact with the Solar Trak instrument panel?"

"I got that directly from the police report. It's public record." It wasn't in the report, but Ken knew nobody at *The Advisor* was fact-checking his pieces. (Or anyone's for that matter.)

"Why don't you just call it the 'patented Solar Trak Guidance System?' Maybe GM's lawyers won't spot that, either."

"They'd be too busy explaining why their patented 'Never Fail' air bag never inflated," Ken came back, now quite sincere in his wide-eyed bewilderment. "Leo, that family bought a mini-van that touts itself as the safest vehicle on the road. And the father watched the cops scrape his daughter off the dashboard because its 'world class Safety Restraint System' failed in three different places."

"You're right. It's criminal."

"It's homicide." Ken thought he was making ground.

"And don't think the father's lawyers won't take GM to town for it. But it's not our job to argue his case." Leo wasn't budging.

"It's a story about corporate negligence and consumer safety."

"It's not a 'story,' Ken. It's 275 words under 'Comings and Goings.' This isn't the New York Times. It's a local paper that lives and dies by its ad sales – especially the ones in the auto section. Get off your high horse." Leo handed back the story.

Yup, real newspapers hate lawsuits. But at *"The American Peephole,"* that wasn't a problem.

❖ ❖ ❖ ❖ ❖

Jerry and Leslie Proud were not your typical couple. Jerry was a Cyber Engineering major at Louisiana Tech in Shreveport when he met a pretty young woman community college student at a wedding reception. Leslie Baker was all of nineteen and a second cousin of the groom. In fact, she'd only met her cousin Benny twice before, the last time at another relative's wedding when she was thirteen. Jerry knew Benny at Tech from the intramural softball team, and after games the two single guys liked to play "wingman" for each other at whatever bar they were getting soused at. Jerry rarely went home with girls, though Benny did somewhat better. In fact, that's how he met and knocked up the bride-to-be. *Poor schmuck*, Jerry thought. *Now he's stuck porking the same piece of ass the rest of his life. While I'm out on the prowl.* Somehow Jerry and Benny's cousin Leslie got seated at the same wedding reception table. Was it a setup? They had no idea.

But the two singles hit it off fairly quickly, and began dating soon after. Leslie loved that Jerry was tall, brilliant, confident, and clean shaven. *Why do all the guys today have to wear the same tired three-day stubble look?* she wondered. *I like to see a man's chin and jawline. If I wanted to kiss a face full of fur, I'd get a goldendoodle.*

Jerry liked that Leslie was not too short, not too skinny, not too moody, and not too popular. He had been dating – or trying to get dates – ever since junior high, but found that most of the girls he was attracted to had little interest in him. But here was a girl that looked nice, smiled at him while he talked, and kept her promises. "I'd love to see you again" meant she really wanted him to call. "I'll meet you at seven" meant she'd be there on time, even if he was fifteen minutes late. (Jerry had a problem with deadlines.) "I've never done this with a boy before" meant she was a virgin – a real one – no ex-boyfriends for her to compare him with. (Jerry had a problem with being compared to other guys. Or other employees. Or anyone to whom he might compare unfavorably, for that matter.)

He wasn't crazy about the fact that she was a devout Presbyterian who dragged him to church almost every Sunday. But it was a small price to pay for regular sex and someone warm to sleep next to at night.

Jerry and Leslie only dated for five months before he popped the question. He was pretty sure she was going to say "yes." You know when a girl is in love with you. But he was still thrown by her answer.

"Yes. As long as it's a covenant marriage."

"I'm…I'm sorry?…" he stammered looking up at her from one knee. "Are you saying yes, or… A covenant marriage?"

"If I get married, I want it to be forever. To you, Jerry. With you."

"Um… yeah, uh… Let me think about that." With that line, Jerry became one of the very few men who'd ever proposed marriage and then told the woman he'd just proposed to, *I'll have to think about it.*

While the idea of a covenant marriage may have been foreign to Jerry Proud, it was an idea that had been gaining traction in the American heartland for some years. A covenant marriage is an arrangement where marrying spouses agree that their marriage will last for the rest of their lives – literally 'til death do us part.' It had started as a religious trend in a small handful of deep red southern states, like Arizona, Arkansas and Louisiana. But after a few high-profile celebrity weddings were promoted as covenant marriages, including an ex-president's daughter – and after a well-organized, well-funded push by the religious right on Twitter and other social media platforms – their popularity began to grow. Eight more states officially recognized them, and there was a pending case in the U.S. Supreme Court as to whether they were even constitutional.

While these so-called "Super Vow" weddings (because like Superman, they were almost impossible to kill) were coming more and more in vogue, the reality of them was not truly as advertised. Though the written covenant the couple signs usually includes language such as, 'Until death shall we part, that no legal apparatus may interfere in these constitutionally protected spiritual vows," most states' laws actually did provide for a covenant marriage divorce in a limited number of situations, including documented adultery, domestic abuse, one spouse committing a felony, or if both spouses have been living separately for two or more years.

Covenant marriages seemed most popular among Evangelicals, Mormons and Catholics. But a growing number of Orthodox and conservative Jews were also opting for them as well. They weren't as common as prenups, but they were catching up.

Ken Feldman knew that well. He had cut his

teeth at the *Boston Advisor* writing a series of features about covenant marriages when they were just gaining public attention. His piece on the rise in domestic abuse reports in covenant marriages got him nominated for a Pulitzer, though he lost to a female *NY Times* reporter who wrote an exposé on black-on-black racism in the WNBA. *What does that even mean,* Ken groused to himself upon hearing the news. *Here I write a piece exposing how organized religion coerces young newlyweds into violently abusive marriages under the guise of morality, and she wins for whining about how light-skinned black players are rude to dark-skinned players.* Ken thought if he had published the piece at the Times or the Post, he'd have won for sure. But he was just a benchwarmer in the journalism game. Pulitzer Prizes go to the 'starters' in life.

As Ken's reporting had discovered, the legal exceptions for spousal abuse and other potential reasons for divorce were hardly ever advantaged by a woman trapped in a horrible covenant marriage. Those women had usually pushed for the covenant in the first place, and found it both confusing and humiliating that they were being tortured by the super vows they thought would guarantee them marital bliss. Plus, they worried they'd become pariahs in their religious community if they broke the ironclad wedding vows they had voluntarily chosen to take.

The piece not only garnered Ken the attention of his journalistic peers, but it garnered him dozens of death threats from religious zealots who thought the article made him a God-hating heretic. He even had to go into hiding for a few months, moving him to purchase his first and only handgun just in case. Ken could not believe how close the far edges of the American fundamentalist movement had come to the Taliban. Any sincere questioning of their practices or motives was reason for death threats and maybe attempts as well.

Like an Olympic gymnast who falls on a landing and suffers the 'twisties,' Ken soon found he was gun-shy about taking on controversial subjects and eventually moved into tabloid journalism, where the only people who got violently angry at you were pampered movie stars and gutless talent agents.

One of the people who had read Ken's piece on covenant marriages was Tom Reiner, a high school guidance counselor in Downey, California, a sleepy bedroom community twenty-five miles southwest of L.A. Tom was a quiet man of faith, and what he saw in the halls and grounds of his high school made him both sick and angry. Kids are slipping, losing respect for the institutions that made this country great! Drowning in moral depravity and high-tech debauchery. Too much texting, too little praying. He saw it in the other teachers, too. Women and men who were God-awful role models for the young people they are charged with molding.

Tom thought covenant marriages might be just the elixir for a society teetering on the cliff's edge of Hell. *Fuck this Ken Feldick guy! If he can't see the obvious good in a lifetime vow of fidelity and commitment, he's part of the problem, not the solution.*

Another person who would have liked to read Ken's exposé on covenant marriages was Jerry Proud. But living in Utah at the time, Jerry never saw Ken's *Boston Advisor* article. And though he had grave reservations about a super vow wedding, Jerry wanted Leslie and Leslie wanted a covenant.

They were married in December of 2010. Within three years Jerry was fantasizing about other women.

Three more years after that he was fantasizing about divorce.

Two years after that he was fantasizing about

murder.

◆ ◆ ◆ ◆ ◆

There it was in print, for all the world to see:

THE AMERICAN PEEPHOLE
(Your eyes in Hollywood)

Myra to Derek: "Bye-Bye, Love!"
*Myra dumps hubby after Derek asks Ian
to "keep an eye" on her.*

For four dollars and ninety-five cents, plus
tax, you can read about the failed relationship and
sexual carnage of America's favorite couple. So
what if it was based on questionable sources? A
little conjecture? It only highlights the hard facts.
They can sue all they want, but Ian Braydon and
Myra Dreyer were not going to bully their way out
of this news story. Their high-profile relationship,
all fourteen months of it, had crashed and burned,
and now it was bleeding out in the tabloids.

Ever since Ian Braydon ended his romance
with ice cream heiress Donna Carvel he was
rumored to be the poster boy for infidelity. And in
Hollywood, that's saying a lot. Ian was known to

have ejaculated a path through some of L.A.'s most famous bedrooms. The more married the actress, the longer Ian seemed to pursue her. Not that any of his pursuits took that long. An extended courtship was probably three dinners. The most widely publicized romance was with the newlywed wife of Ian's best friend, Derek Chase, the kid he roomed with at Yale Drama School and through most of their lean years in Hollywood. Both had broken fast in the movie business, first with a low-budget, Indy picture they wrote for themselves that won some film festivals and critical acclaim. Then each moved on to studio pictures that quickly built up their images and their price tags. By the time Ian and Derek won their Golden Globe for best screenplay, they were heirs-apparent to the "old Hollywood" of Hanks and Cruise and Damon and Affleck.

The addition of a stunningly sexy 23-year old actress named Myra Dreyer to their circle gave them the aura of the Rat Pack, Hollywood's highest accolade. *The American Peephole* was awash with stories of Derek and Myra's torrid on-set romance and made buddy shots of the three best pals a weekly fixture on its covers. At every event worth covering, there were the three amigos, arm-in-arm like Dorothy, the Scarecrow and the Tin Man prancing down their very own, very public Yellow Brick Road. When Derek finally popped the question to Myra, the plans for their lavish Malibu wedding and the six hundred name guest list demanded its own separate, special edition.

Three months after the very public private affair, Derek got a call to shuttle to The Philippines for a part in Scorsese's latest project. It would be Derek's first starring role and a part Ian himself had lobbied for, the first visible fissure in their much-ballyhooed friendship. But the two Yale alums buried the hatchet over a few bourbons and Derek asked his former roomie to "keep an eye on Myra" until he was back stateside.

"Maybe take her out to dinner once or twice," Derek asked. "Keep her mind off things."

"My pleasure," Ian grinned with all the irony he knew the promise would come to mean.

Derek wasn't gone two nights before Ian was banging Myra. And he must've put in more than his usual effort, because Myra never looked back. They were shacking up by the next weekend, and doing the town very publicly to boot. You'd think a married woman carousing around with her husband's best friend/best man would be a little camera shy. Not Myra. It was as if she was dressing for the paparazzi – showing up in front of the most public restaurants in her Paris best, accessorized with Ian's arms as a belt. Her agents told her it was bad for her image. But Myra was all of 23, and the only image she cared about was Ian's naked body doing her from behind in his wall-to-wall mirrored bedroom.

Ken was one of the first reporters to break the story, though by the time *The Peephole* showed up on supermarket stands that Tuesday, it was old news. Most papers wrote that Myra and Ian had become an item within hours after Derek had landed in the Philippines. But Ken Feldman was the only reporter to write about the pre-flight covenant between the two Yale pals and Ian's sexual duplicity. Ken's jealous peers in the mainstream media labeled his story a cheap embellishment, a low blow at Ian taken not to hurt him, but solely to one-up the legitimate news media. How could any reputable news outlet report a private, two person conversation that was attributed to only one unnamed source?

What they didn't know – what no one could even guess – was just how reliable that unnamed source was. Ian often called Ken Feldman with a bit of self-promoting PR. And what could be better press for a Hollywood stud like Ian than having broken up the duo *People Magazine* once anointed the "sexiest couple alive?"

◆ ◆ ◆ ◆ ◆

"Derek to Ian: 'Keep an eye on her for me." It was scrolled across a full page close-up of Ian tonguing Myra.

Ken's editors at *The Peephole* were thrilled to have a legitimate scoop on the rest of the world. The papers were flying off the racks, and the rest of the celebrity gossip industry could only try to play catch up. But Ken took little pride in his spoon-fed scoop. What troubled him, the real mystery that lay out there for him or someone else to uncover, was the "whys" of the story. Here was a gorgeous, fabulously rich 23-year-old woman hitched to one of the sexiest men on earth. Everything was in place for a fantasy marriage. What made her chuck all that for another guy?

Was Derek abusive? Cheating on her? Bad in bed? Or was he everything he seemed to be, but Ian was just that much more desirable? Ken was obsessed with such questions. He had probably gotten into celebrity muckraking out of some void in his own social life, which consisted of a handful of short, painful sexual dalliances that passed for relationships. Even at 36, though he'd fallen for several women by this age, Ken didn't know if he'd ever experienced the kind of passion you see in movies...or on the pages of *"The Peephole."* And he was quite sure he'd never won the heart of a woman the way these famous guys do so effortlessly and often. What could make a woman like Myra, who was so clearly infatuated and beguiled by Derek at one point, one-eighty and drop her ideal man for another guy?

Instead of sleeping at night, Ken would ponder the riddle for hours. Did Myra secretly have a crush on Ian? One that maybe she could barely admit to herself until Derek was 7,300 miles out of the picture? Or did she say yes to his dinner invitation thinking it would be one more night out among friends, only to be caught off-guard by his sensual charisma and his unyielding attention only to her?

Ken imagined them in a booth at Spago, at first amused by the gawking masses, soaking up their beautiful energy while wondering when the missing piece of the celebrity puzzle would appear. But moments into the meal, Myra would be overtaken by another, more primitive sensation: that she was being seduced. It would begin with long, uninterrupted gazes into her eyes, along with Ian's charming banter. Maybe a shared intimate secret and laugh. Maybe the whispering touch of a hand. It was all innocent, the warmth of a good friend opening up to her without the distraction of her always-present husband. But washed over the innocence was a layer of sexual excitement. The unspoken realization of the mating advances of yet another perfect man.

Do women think like that, Ken wondered as his head shifted on the pillow. Was she bowled over by the mere attention of a man, however perfect and powerful his intimate desires were? Or did Myra seduce Ian?

True, Ian had told Ken that afternoon about the favor Derek had asked of him, indicating that he already had plans to turn that favor into ashes. But maybe she had an agenda of her own, one that coincidently (or not so coincidently) led them both back to his bed for the night and for the duration.

Ken fantasized about that night. Did they start before they were at his place? Did she know she was going to sleep with him? He imagined Ian and her acknowledging the sexual event that was about to take place. Did a man like Ian Braydon really have to seduce a woman? Did he have to make a move or worry about rejection? Ken didn't know. Maybe they had even flirted with the notion days or weeks before. Maybe a touch or a hug that went unnoticed by Derek but spoke volumes to them. But Ken didn't like to think so. He imagined a night of pure sexual virginity. A night where a beautiful woman would enter an apartment as the lover of one man, but emerge the sexual slave of another. It made Ken hard.

How good could Ian have been? His physique was taught and smooth, that much everyone knew from his films. The smile golden and radiant. The charisma frighteningly powerful. But the man she was married to was no slouch, either. Maybe she started out with a curiosity – a mere weakness of the flesh that she hoped to douse with little or no consequence. One dance on the passion pole before pledging herself back to her true love for all eternity. But once enveloped in Ian, suddenly the world seemed different.

Was Ian really that good? Not being a woman, Ken could only surmise. So many women had given themselves to Ian, and so many marriages torn asunder in his path. Could his skills as a lover be so advanced as to be in a league by himself? And what "skills" would that be? Endurance? Unselfishness? A touch or a technique that drives a woman beyond the bounds she had previously known? Or was it simply the product of a pheromone high that is endemic in the nature of philandering? The intoxicating combo of danger and taboo that heightens the sensual senses beyond anything previously experienced?

Yup, Ken was consumed by his erotic curiosity. Like the rest of the world, when it came to Ian and Myra and Derek, he had to know more.

Luckily, Ken was paid for that curiosity. Which meant he could afford to indulge it. It seduced him, and he gave himself willingly.

Derek returned from the Philippines ready to do battle for his woman. He called and texted and emailed and stalked Myra for weeks. But nothing he could say or do or buy her could win her back. She told him she had fallen in love with Ian and they were even talking about marriage.

Which meant she would need a divorce from Derek.

Derek bitched and cried to anyone who would listen. Even to Ken Feldman, whom he'd gotten to know a bit over the years. But none of it was bringing his wayward wife back to his bed. So after a few more months of stewing as he watched the news coverage of Myra and Ian tooling around L.A. like honeymooners on parade, he finally took his agents' advice and moved on. They told him that interviews of him pining after his cheating wife were damaging his box office numbers and his career. Even Scorsese had called Derek's agent to complain about what the image of a cuckolded leading man was doing to his new film.

So Derek started dating. And dating. And doing two girls at a time. And three. If Myra Dreyer didn't want him, most American women did, and he dove into the dating pool cannonball style. Any hot woman who smiled at him at an event or in a drug store might end up in his bed. Or his jacuzzi. Or just blowing him in the drug store stockroom. Pretty soon he had gotten over Myra…somewhat. He still secretly pined for her and remembered how good it felt to pull her legs around him.

But Myra was gone forever. So he signed the divorce settlement, which was fairer to him than California state law would have been, thanks to the prenup they had signed. No alimony, and he kept his Pacific Palisades house (Myra had her own in Silver Lake that she hadn't sold yet) and his collection of classic sports cars, even though Myra bought two of the cars for him as gifts. She got the twenty-five grand worth of Peloton gym equipment, the Pilates reformer, the art collection (most of which she'd picked out), and their beagle, Shemp. Beyond Myra, Shemp was what Derek missed most.

Maybe most important of all, he kept their close friends. That wasn't in the prenup, but people who knew them best thought Derek was the clear victim in the breakup.

The only close friend he didn't keep was Ian.

Ian and Myra were now the dynamic duo of Hollywood, just as Ian and Derek had once been.

But what Derek didn't know was that while Myra was falling deeper and deeper in love with her new paramour, the feelings weren't mutual. Like all young boys who can eat as much candy as they want, Ian's sweet tooth was getting a little bored with the same flavor every day and night. Myra was okay, but there's a whole world of young, tight bodies out there just waiting to give themselves to a movie star.

Ian wanted the brass ring. And Myra's once-dazzling sheen was fading.

Chapter 2

"*S*o? Should I get married or not?"

Tom Reiner was still daydreaming as the question pulled him back into the room. "That's a hard question for me – for anyone – to answer, Alicia. I think you have to look inside your – "

"Oh, cut the shit, Mr. Reiner."

Her words were barely audible over Reiner's inner monologue. *Alicia Strandquest is not the most charming twelfth grader you've ever met. How she found anyone to sleep with her, let alone knock her up, is beyond me. Sure, the chest is nice – all teenaged girls have firm racks. But the rest of her looks positively anorexic, though the few extra pregnancy pounds have diminished her –*

"Should I marry Salvador or not? Come on, Mr. R. You're the guidance counselor. Where's the freaking guidance?"

"First of all, watch your language in here, young lady. That piece of guidance you've been given before." Mr. Reiner wasn't the toughest disciplinarian at Downey High; everyone knew that. His faux stern rebukes usually came off more as a man close to tears. But he still tried to project an air of authority or severity or control – or something. It came with the territory. "Now you know well and good that the type of guidance I'm here to dispense has nothing to do with the question you're asking. You want to pick a college, choose a major? I'm here to help. And I can certainly sympathize with your predica–"

"Great. Thanks. That's just what I need." The teenager exhaled a big pink bubble and let it pop onto her purple lipstick, then sucked it back in. Alicia was a tough crowd, all by herself. "So what's a good major for an unwed teen mother who can barely pay for her morning Starbucks?"

"Okay, right there, I can give you some advice. Caffeine isn't good for a pregnant woman. Or the baby. Definitely. So you should cut out the Starbucks right off the bat." Reiner knew he was coming off as an idiot. But he was so flustered. He never felt comfortable with teenaged girls to begin with; their overt sexuality was so foreign to him. He realized six years ago that being a high school guidance counselor was probably the worst line of work a man like him could have gone into, a thought that paralyzed him daily. *All these sexually charged nymphomaniacs fluttering through the halls and the parking lots. Prancing through his office umpteen times a day, asking where they should go to college or how to get in one. Like they're going to do anything in college but spread their legs for every jock or frat boy that –*

"I mean, Salie doesn't want any part of getting married. That much he made quite clear. But I know if I tell his dad what he's done…"

"Now you listen to me, young lady." On this, Mr. Reiner's ire was authentic and convincing. "Marriage is not a game. You do not blackmail or coerce someone into marriage. Even if you're pregnant, which by the way is no one's fault but your own." *Good, she's not interrupting. I must be landing with her on some level.* "Now, I know your mom and dad. They're fine, decent people. And while I don't know Salvador's parents as well, I'm sure…"

"His mom's dead." Alicia snapped out another pink bubble for effect.

"Oh. I'm sorry." *Who am I consoling? Just another stupid comment. Keep going. Maybe she won't notice.* "My point is, marriage is a sacred thing. It may have lost some of its reverence in this country these last few, well, longer than you've been alive. But when I was young we were taught to respect the institution of holy matrimony. Anything less is a mortal sin."

"Oh, pu-lease. Don't go all pontiff on me, Mr. Reiner. If I wanted that, I'd go to confession or something."

"This is not about religion."

"Right. On that, we agree. It's not about being Catholic or holy institutions or mortal sin or any of those things I know you live for." Alicia knew she was due north on that point; everyone knew that Mr. Reiner was a pious Jesus freak. *You'd think that would'a kept him from even getting a job teaching in a public high school, what with the separation of church and state and the like. He must'a lied about it on his application,* was all she could figure. "It's about my life, and how do I rescue it from the trash bin. I mean, let's get real here. Me. A baby. No husband. No high school degree. Do the math."

"And would you be any better off if you could get Salvador to marry you? I mean, if you want to be 'real.' How long would a shotgun marriage like that last?"

"How long do any marriages last these days? Look at Mrs. Gillespie."

"We'll not delve into the personal lives of the faculty here. Though maybe that is part of my point," Reiner mused with total conviction. *The behavior of the faculty around here is such a poor excuse for role models,* he thought. *Especially a woman like Spanish teacher Maria Gillespie. But maybe in some perverse way her abominable extra-marital antics can be a lesson to one of these kids.* "Even the best intentions of mature adults can lead to a disastrous marriage. You want to be a divorced mother? You think that's any better?"

"Yeah. At least you get alimony."

"Oh yes. Salvador Mencia is good for a whole lot of alimony."

"So you do have an opinion," Alicia said getting up. "I shouldn't marry him. All I needed to know." She flung her backpack over her emaciated left shoulder.

"I didn't say that!" Reiner knew that the wrong advice – the wrong choice of words offered to a teenaged girl, especially in this situation – was a recipe for a sexual harassment charge. "You have to do what is in your heart, what is right for you. I'm just trying to illustrate all the factors that go into – "

"With you, that makes five adults who think it'd be a mistake." As she shot out a blue-nailed index finger. "My Aunt Judy…." Then a pink-nailed middle finger. "Her boyfriend." Then a silver-nailed ring finger. "You…" Then an orange-nailed pinky. "The doctor at the abortion clinic. Bitch." She paused. "Oh! And you'll be quite pleased to hear, Mrs. Gillespie also thinks I'm better off without him."

On that, her green-tipped thumb joined the crowd. "Guess that's unanimous, huh?"

"If that's your sample universe." He was momentarily speechless in the presence of such logic. "But why solicit so many opinions?"

Alicia shrugged. "Strength in numbers?" She stood up and scrunched a bye-bye wave. "Later."

Tom watched her almost skip out of his office, and he finally breathed. *Another child doomed to a modern life. Something has to be done.*

As Tom moved around his desk, he thought of all the times he'd said that to himself. "Something has to be done." He was a devout man. A man of God. He spent many a Sunday morning at mass. He had even worked with young people, both in his day job and at Sunday school in Bible class.

But it was too little, too few. *Something has to be done*, Tom thought. That afternoon, Tom Reiner set out to really do something.

$14.95 a month for boob puppets?! Jerry Proud hated this kind of porn. When he ordered The Bachelor Channel (TBC) last spring, his assumption was he'd be able to see a little action any time of the day or night. *That's what soft-core porn is supposed to be, right? People doing it. Shower sex...bathtub sex...kitchen sex...SEX. People having s-e-x.* But ever since he signed up at fourteen-ninety-five a month, he'd been disappointed more than he'd been pleased. Talk shows about sex. Courtroom comedies about sex. Faux reality series about sex. Even this show, a tongue-in-cheek "children's" series called "Candy's Birds 'N Bees Playhouse" with talking faces painted on fake boobs. But not enough hot, raw s-e-x.

And when there was a little bit of action, it was usually the sex he was least interested in. Lots of lesbian stuff. Jerry could live without that. There was something oddly uncomfortable about watching a woman get off on another woman, which he found more intimidating than hot. Three ways – those always looked so fake. Inter-racial sex – also intimidating. And the worst: masturbation. *Why do men* – Jerry presumed it was men who programmed TBC – *why do they assume anyone wants to watch a woman fingering herself. They would never presume to show a man jerking off on camera.* Thank God for that, Jerry thought. That would be the day he canceled the service for good.

"It's so simple," Jerry mumbled as he bit into his tuna sandwich, "guys and girls making love." Jerry didn't talk to himself often. Usually only when he was mad at the TV or the car radio. Jerry used to talk to talk radio a lot when he was on the road.

The long stretches between Las Vegas and his sales territory in Arizona and New Mexico made him unusually fatigued, and a dose of some local, bleeding-heart liberal ha-hoo blasting the newly elected president really yanked Jerry's chain. "Not every problem known to mankind can be traced to the Oval Office," he'd rant back, defending the devout Evangelical Christian president that Jerry had enthusiastically voted for the past November.

He'd listen some more to his far-left counterpart as they hammered the new Commander in Chief for the latest foreign policy debacle or Texas's new and very controversial covenant marriage law. Then it was Jerry's turn again. "You wanna lay the fall of Peru at his feet? So be it. Or the recession that hit three months into his first term? Fine. The disturbing uptick in sex trafficking and the lack of progress in the war on gender selection, make your case. But laying state by state Covenant Laws on him, that's going three bridges too far." Commercial break.

Of course, these days Jerry mostly worked out of his home office – the tiny, lime green guest bedroom in his Las Vegas home that Leslie let him convert into an office so he could cut down on his travel days. It also cut down on their income, but Leslie's part-time waitressing job at the MGM Grand kept them afloat. Jerry wished she'd find a full-time gig that would bring in more income. Then he could really kick back. But until Megan and Luke were out of elementary school, Leslie had this "thing" about being home at 2:45 for them.

So, until the twins were safely into junior high, Jerry had to work the phones and still hit the road about ten days a month. It wasn't an easy sell to Randy, his boss, who didn't like the idea of one of his regional reps working out of his house. But he also didn't like having Jerry around the office too much; something about Jerry made Randy vaguely uncomfortable these days. And it wasn't just Nashville. Randy knew Nashville was bullshit. *A poor working guy can't even look sideways at a woman anymore, let alone tell a harmless joke in her presence.* It was Jerry's constant ranting at the toaster oven about politics that concerned him. Specifically the covenant laws. That's what made Randy most uncomfortable. *No one likes the new covenant laws spreading from state to state,* he figured. *No one likes speeding tickets or taxes, either, but you don't have to bitch about them every single day.*

But Jerry had this tunnel vision about the evils of super vows. He had been pressured into signing one of those covenant things, and he regrets it every single day. Now he saw other men being coerced into signing away their lives, and he hated it. *A man should be free to get married as many times as he likes, to as many women as he likes,* he would proselytize in the break room. *Women too. Like that Myra chick. She wants to bang her husband's best friend, that's her business. She wants to do me? I'm there – covenant or not.* As if a woman like Myra Dreyer would want a sweaty slob like Jerry Proud.

But Jerry would go on and on, and Randy could see it was making the female employees uncomfortable. The last thing he needed this quarter was a harassment suit. So when Jerry asked if he could focus more on cold calls and work from home three days a week, Randy jumped at it. "Great idea, Jer. You generate leads, and I'll get some kid out of college to run himself ragged on the road."

Jerry felt like he'd just won the jackpot. So did Randy.

Tom Reiner approached the administration office like a man possessed. Most days, he dreaded going to work. But today he was not just a guidance counselor, he was a man in motion.

Tom had spent most of last night fiddling with his computer, trying to print out the perfect flyer to grab people's attention. He wasn't necessarily the best copywriter in the world, but for a high school guidance counselor he thought it was more than adequate.

Teachers 4 Matrimony!

Help foster a new respect for marriage and commitment among our students. Come to the 3:15 meeting and help bring back *fidelity, faith and family values* to our curriculum and our lives.

RSVP: Mr. Reiner
Office of Student Guidance
by 1:00 pm today.

Tom was fairly pleased with the font and colors, though he wasn't 100% sure the name was a keeper. And was "fidelity, faith and family values" too much alliteration? Tom could second-guess himself to death. But it was too late now. Today was the day.

Tom found an empty place on the cork board. Well, not *empty* empty, but he moved a few notices around – nobody needs another reminder about the monthly CPR refresher course – and he pinned up his flyer in the center for all to see.

"What's this? A new club?"

Tom didn't have to turn to know the soft voice coming from Miss Yoeste, the Geometry teacher. But he turned and acted surprised anyway. "Well, no, Sandra. Not a club, per se. I'm hoping to organize – galvanize – the faculty to help bring a sense of family values back to the student population around here."

Tom always had a thing for Sandy Yoeste. Late 30s, yes, but she could pass for a decade younger. *Not frumpy like the rest of the female faculty. With the exception of that whore, Mrs. Gillespie,* Tom fumed to himself. *But she's another story entirely.*

"Is this sanctioned," Miss Yoeste asked. "The only reason I ask is, I thought Mrs. Angler was quite clear about religious clubs meeting on school grounds."

"Well, again, it's not a 'club.' And I don't believe it's 'religious' in the strictest sense. I mean, don't we as teachers have a responsibility to bring morality and values to the kids we teach every day? If not us, who? If not now, when?"

"Here, here," smiled Miss Yoeste as she applauded his mini-speech. "If it's sanctioned, you can put me down."

"Great! It's a date." *Oh Jesus, did that really come out of my mouth?!* "I mean, of course, I look forward to seeing you…and the rest of the faculty… there."

"What room?" Miss Yoeste's voice was soft

as a pillow.

"Hmmm?"

"The meeting. What's the room number?"

Oh crap! I forgot to put down the room number?" "Two-oh-seven," he blushed back. Tom grabbed for the Magic Marker hanging from a string tied to the board and wrote it on the bottom of the flyer, destroying its carefully crafted aesthetic appeal. "Room 207. Three-fifteen."

"I'll be there," she promised in that lovely voice.

Tom nodded. Miss Yoeste smiled and moved off to her mail slot.

The room number! Dammit! Think, you moron!! Think!!!

◆ ◆ ◆ ◆ ◆

Eleven-forty-seven. Damn it! A two-hour HBO movie, a half hour of news, *The Tonight Show* monolog, and Jerry was still nowhere near falling asleep for the night.

"Come on…turn it off and go to bed." The voice came from under a pillow, where Leslie Proud tried to shelter herself from the light and sound of the TV, as she did every night.

"I am in bed."

"What time is it?" Leslie poked her head out like a turtle in a REM state.

"I don't know. Go back to sleep."

"I haven't *been* to sleep. Are you okay?" Leslie was genuinely worried about her husband these days. Barely sleeps, moody, sharp with the kids. And with her.

"I'm fine. I'll turn it down."

"Honey, the light. It's bad enough you aren't sleeping. But if I don't sleep, my morning is hell."

"Well. Heaven forbid *your* morning should be hell. After all, pouring coffee and slinging hash is so much more important than what I do every day."

"I didn't say that. But you do have a little more flexibility as to when you get out of bed."

"Because I have no office to go to. Right?" Jerry hated her passive aggressive crap.

"I didn't say that." Leslie looked at him staring straight ahead at the TV. "Just don't read all night, okay?"

Jerry clicked the side button on the phone, launching the room into darkness.

"Thanks. 'Night, sweetie." She kissed him on the cheek and rolled back to sleep.

And Jerry stared. What to think about? Think. Something pleasant, something hopeful.

Inheriting some money. Right...like anyone in his family has two cents to leave to him. The new BMW convertible. Not on their take-home. They can barely afford their crummy used VW van.

That's the problem with marriage, Jerry thought. It kills your dreams. Jerry remembered when he was a kid, and he could dream of playing professional baseball someday. But as you age, that dream becomes tarnished by reality, just around the time most boys discover girls. Then of course, you spend the next 10, 15, 20 years dreaming about sex...where to get it, how to get more of it, how great it would be to get it with someone other than the person you're screwing right now. Sure, there are the parallel dreams that come and go – career, status, wealth...maybe even making that Oscar night acceptance speech that turns every preconceived notion everyone ever had about you on its head.

But those are fleeting flights of fancy, changing with every new stage of your life, and even those dreams are mere pitstops on the road to getting laid. Win the lottery? What would you do? Quit your job? Buy some toys? Move to an island? Then what? Dump the wife and bang a hula girl. Become a rock star? Dump the wife and bang groupies. Elected president? Ignore the first lady and bang starlets and interns. It's the evergreen of the ego – the one dream that endures through the years – wild, new sex with a young, tight, perfect body. It becomes you, it permeates every fantasy, it's ingrained in your nervous system.

Then boom, suddenly one day you're married and you're supposed to stop thinking about it. Simply expected to stop wanting it. You and your spouse fall into a ritual of lovemaking, a pattern that has to become, at some level, routine. If not downright monotonous. It's not a question of falling out of love, although that's a typical side-effect. It's simply, hey, the most exciting part was always the hunt...the seduction. Will we do it tonight? How do I get from kiss to nudity to penetration without objections? Will she feel different than other women? Better? Tighter? Hotter? Will I be better with her than I am with other women? Harder? Stronger? Longer? Will I make her come harder, quicker, more often? Will I spoil her for other men? Will I be her Ian? Will she be my Myra? Will the next woman I bed be my one great fuck of a lifetime?

With a wife, those intriguing questions are forever silenced. Even the hottest sexual relationship has to diminish. They never get hotter. New is only new once. And Jerry isn't even sure he and Leslie were ever all that hot. Sure, the early days had their great moments. And even now, she is still sexy and knows how to turn him on. Passion, yes. But fire? Sparks? Come on. Eleven years. Now it's about bodily functions. "Keeping your joints waxed," as Jerry liked to joke.

So if you're not fantasizing about sex, what does a guy think about? What does he hope for? Wish for? Live for? For his kids? Seeing them graduate and get married? That's just too far off. For their safety and happiness? Sure, you want that, but it's not the stuff of fantasy. What else? Career advancement? Not every occupation lends itself to "climbing the ladder." You don't go from software salesman to CEO of a Fortune 500 company. Jerry had started as a programmer and was pretty good at writing code; he even did a little amateur hacking back in his college days, just for fun. But once he started competing for work with young kids from the Ivy League schools, Jerry saw the dead-end of his programming days heading like a locomotive right at him. So he switched to software sales, figuring he could be his own "boss" on the road and be the master of his fate. Ha! Fate indeed.

What Jerry became was a high-tech Willy Lohman, and success for him would be measured in how long he can stay on the road and keep eking out a living. It's a grueling lifestyle that sometimes demands weeks on the road, with five-to-ten hour drives between the handful of clients he services. What then, retirement? In his business, you retire when you can't sell anymore. It's not a golden ring to be grabbed, it's a disease to be avoided. Even if he could back out gracefully with a few bucks in his pocket, Jerry wasn't a golfer or the type of guy who was gonna build a boat and sail the world. Retirement was a punishment, as far as he was concerned.

And if he were to luck out, win a lottery or something, what would that change? Early retirement? He'd just be Jerry Proud with no job and no financial worries, and even more time to fill with no fantasies to fill it. (Plus, if Leslie quit her job and stayed home full-time, it'd mean more stress on their marriage, not less.) A bigger house? He likes the one he has. Sports cars? What's a sports car except a way to attract chicks? Travel the world? With Leslie? That is not a recipe for happiness.

Look, who are we kidding? Happiness is a twenty-two year old 5'9 supermodel. Period. It's instinct. Men are made to 1) provide, and 2) promulgate the species. Providing isn't fun. Promulgating is.

Like 'Ms. McKenzie-Jenrette-Wallace,' the perky Asian receptionist at a client's company (McKenzie-Jenrette-Wallace) who Jerry liked to flirt with when there on sales calls. Without Leslie in the picture, Jerry would be free to go back to Macon and hook up with her. She might not be interested, but maybe she might. Another sales call, "accidentally" running into her – "Remember me?" – a few flirtatious jokes, dinner, champagne. Pretty soon they are at her place. "Coming up for a cup of coffee, Jer?" Jerry would know what she really wanted. His arms around her waist. His hands on the inside of her tight thigh. Her dark tan skin twitching as she moves his hand up under her skirt...

Within minutes, Jerry came in his hand. Minutes after that, he was asleep.

Chapter 3

"*Kenneth* Farmington," Ken Feldman lied. "F-A-R-M – "

"I know how to spell it, sir. It's not on the list." The doorman had danced this dance before. Lots of people come to Sky Bar with an attitude, thinking that's going to get them through the door. But a bouncer at a Hollywood club learns how to sift through the B.S. and the 'tude to figure out who really belongs and who is just trying to asshole their way in. This guy Farmington was clearly the later. *Kenneth Farmington*, he thought. *Sounds gay.*

Ken stood in front of the 6'5" set of rippling muscles that pass for a person, confident that he could out-talk/out-think/out-play this goon and his 48" pecs. After all, Ken was one of the most important reporters in Hollywood. He should just walk up to the velvet ropes and be escorted in, like the sickeningly gorgeous and powerful people who were happily dancing and flirting inside. But tonight, Ken was incognito, traveling under an assumed name. You see, the name Ken Feldman doesn't muster a lot of warmth and compassion in L.A. these days. Not after some of the bylines Ken had registered over the past two years. In fact, if he tried to get into a place like Sky Bar using his proper surname, he'd probably be let in with his name announced just so a few of the Neanderthal patrons could punch him out and toss him curbside themselves. So when Ken wanted to get some usable material, he always went undercover. He purposely chose to use his real first name, "Kenneth," so he would be able to respond if anyone who did know him said hello. And it has the added benefit of sounding vaguely gay, which somehow carried extra cache in these types of places.

He chose "Farmington" because it was a tad haute, and sounded less ethnic than "Feldman," which Ken despised. God, could any name have brought him more derision and unhappiness these last 36 years than "Feldman"? Might as well just be named "Jewboy."

Ken had taken pains to make sure he was on the list. He'd called Jeffery Stanholt at Paramount to make sure he was on. Jeffery owed him after the piece Ken wrote about the animal cruelty controversy on Stanholt's last picture. *Who knows why those two horses really died on the set,* Ken reasoned. *But attributing it to a cocaine overdoes was inspired!* His readers slurped up the bizarre idea that two stunt horses could somehow crane their heads through the window of an actor's trailer and snort his fifty-thousand dollar stash. And when the actor in question is Ian Braydon, it takes on an air of surreal believability. Or at least as believable as the alternate scenario floating around town – that the horses wiped out in a mock parachute jump the director improvised on the set. Paramount had a big vested interest in quelling that story. After all, who's gonna go see a movie that killed two horses by giddy-yapping them out of a C-130 at four thousand feet.

But convince people that the stunt horses met some metaphoric Hollywood fate at the hands of illegal drugs and the audience will show up in droves. True or not (and Ken suspected it wasn't), the story took the heat off the director and had the added plus of making Ian seem somehow even more depraved than he already was. Anyway, it was enough of a red herring to keep the ASPCA from demanding an investigation and kept Paramount's big summer release from being killed by bad press. Imagine, two horses OD on a movie set and it's *not* bad press! Only in Hollywood.

So these days when Ken calls Stanholt's office for a favor – get me into that party, get my name on this VIP list – he never has to ask twice. But tonight someone apparently dropped the ball – Stanholt's ditzy assistant, no doubt – and he was stuck on line with the peons who had no hope of ever getting inside.

"Could you look under 'Feldman'," Ken mumbled in total embarrassment.

"Feldman?" The doorman glared. *Anti-Semite!* Ken glared back with a meek smile. "I got a 'Ken Feldman'," he pointed at the list, his pecs almost ripping through the sleeve of his black T-shirt as he flexed. "Plus one."

"That's me. The girl must have called it in wrong."

The doorman squinted his eyes. "How do you get 'Feldman' from 'Farmington'?"

Oh great, I have to debate with Pec Man. Shit! "You don't. You don't get 'Feldman' from 'Farmington' unless you're a complete dip-shit idiot who keeps confusing me with a character from our Christmas release. I'm the 'Ken Farmington' who produced the movie. She's got me mixed up with 'Ken Feldman,' a fictional character from that movie. Trust me, when she called in 'Feldman,' she meant me."

The doorman glared for a few more seconds. It was one of the weakest arguments anyone had ever made. So weak that maybe, just maybe, this guy is really on the up. In which case, he didn't need his boss giving him shit tomorrow about turning away some bigwig homo movie producer. He unlatched the rope and grudgingly nodded Ken through.

"Thank you," Ken called back without looking. He was in.

Like most secular people following the news these days, Jerry Proud was concerned as he read about the tidal wave of state covenant laws in the works. He understood that marriage is not about love; it's a financial contract between two people. And that contract is governed by the laws in the state of your residence. Smart people grasp this concept and take control of their own destinies. Some, like Derek and Myra, sign a prenup, which makes untangling a messy marriage less complicated. But some, like Jerry and Leslie, sign a covenant, which makes untangling a messy marriage almost impossible.

Jerry knew for a while that he and Leslie didn't have much of a future together. Their sex life had come to a virtual standstill, and most days they only saw each other briefly in the morning or at night. Then there were his travel days for work. Though physically hard on him, the emotional respite of not having to be polite to his ball-and-chain had become a welcomed reprieve. But since he started staying home three days a week, he no longer had that luxury. He missed his road freedom.

Not that Jerry was any big player, mind you. Besides his secret, late-night trysts with The Bachelor Channel, he had remained totally faithful to his wife for eleven years. He was proud of that. It's not like Jerry didn't have his chances.

There was that Asian receptionist at McKenzie-Jenrette-Wallace that seemed real friendly whenever he made a client visit. No ring, nice legs, very shy. He could've asked her to dinner. She would've smiled at first and probably made a joke about his wedding ring. But he was on the road, just a lonely software salesman in need of some pleasant dinner conversation. What's the harm? She'd finally give in and say yes. He'd meet her at the bar of his hotel, buy her a drink, make her laugh, then casually mention that his room has free cable and ask if she ever watches "erotic movies." Of course, she'd demure – no woman admits that at first. Leslie wouldn't even admit liking fuck flicks until six years into their marriage, he mused. And look at her now. She even tapes her favorite TBC shows for those rare times when she's in the mood. *Crap! Stop thinking about Leslie.* Jerry could feel his erection softening under his sandwich plate.

Back to the hotel bar. Another round of drinks, a few more light-hearted but strategically dropped references to erotic fantasies, and Miss McKenzie-Jenrette-Wallace is up in his room. At first she'd be standing by the window admiring the view as he flips on the pay-per-view guide. Jerry would pretend not to know the titles, though he's seen most of them more than once. He'd look for something about cheating...something with a little danger in it... *Ah, here's the one. "Charlotte's Web." The one with the Asian actress – the blond one – perfect!* His guest would identify immediately with a lonely married Asian lady who fantasizes about her husband's hunky step-son. Within a few minutes, Jerry knew, frat boy and step-mom would be going at it good and strong. *In a hot tub*, Jerry believed. Yes, he distinctly remembers her giving her husband's son head in the hot tub. That scene always tickled Jerry. *Can a woman really do that without drowning?* No matter; that was make-believe, and what Jerry had in mind for his Asian beauty was real life.

First, he'd angle her toward the bed. Get her to take off her shoes; crack open a baby vodka bottle from the mini fridge. Then Jerry would surprise her by *not* sitting next to her on the bed. He'd plop down in the lounge chair; making her wonder if he was a closet Boy Scout. Or maybe gay. That was the goal, to both put her at ease but make her want him to make a move.

He had to be cautious, though, especially after Nashville. Jerry couldn't risk another black-eye in his employment file. *Nashville was a tease; she couldn't wait for me to slip up so she could file a complaint and weasel herself a pay raise in the process.* But it had made Jerry very leery around female co-workers. He was lucky Leslie didn't bolt then – two months suspension without pay was more than a mere embarrassment for them; it was a financial body blow – and Jerry knew he had played his one free hand with his spouse. The ten grand in lawyers fees weren't soon forgotten by Leslie, either, yet Jerry knew that was just a drop in the bucket compared to alimony and child support if she left him. Plus, getting thrown out of a covenant marriage would be the ultimate humiliation. So this time he would take every conceivable precaution. No more Nashvilles.

Jerry would wait for the shower scene – he knew this script by heart – until the steam was almost coming out of the 32" flatscreen. That's when Jerry would make his move. He'd slip into the bathroom and turn on his shower. When he came out, she'd be looking at him with a curious, slightly devious smile. He wouldn't speak. Just a smile. A subtle gesture of the hand – *come here*. If she moved to him, he knew it was safe.

Then it happened. Her legs, once casually tucked under her on the bed, unfurled down to the floor. She used her hand to pat out the tiny folds in her skirt, then started to rise. Heading for the door? Oh crap, what was he thinking?! Turning on the shower? How un-cool was that?! Like he could ever explain that to Randy or Mr. Jenrette or Leslie!

Randy would boot his ass in a second. With cause, which means–

But wait…Miss McKenzie-Jenrette-Wallace wasn't heading for the door at all…she was heading for the bathroom! Slipping her hands around Jerry's waist. Their lips melting together as she gently guided him backward onto the tile floor. Steam rising. Shirt tails coming loose. Her right hand slowly sliding down…down…until…

Snow? Oh come on! Where's the damn picture?! Jerry dropped his tuna sandwich on his lap and lunged for the remote. He flipped to CNN. Snow. ESPN. Snow. *Great, one-hundred and eighteen dollars a month and they can't even keep the porn coming uninterrupted for one 24-hour period. Christ! Miss Saigon and frat boy will be out of the shower and dressed by the time this comes back!* Jerry loved fantasizing to that scene. There was something so, well, perfectly erotic in it. Not body parts plowing into body parts. Not butts pounding or legs flailing. Just slow, sensual love making under a rain of steaming hot water. This was what Jerry was paying for, and they couldn't even keep it coming till he was ready.

Just as well. 2:28 a.m. If he doesn't go

downstairs to bed soon, Leslie might come looking for him. *Better just go to bed. Hell, I never would'a got a girl like Miss McKenzie-Jenrette-Wallace to my room, anyway.*

Downstairs, Leslie Proud didn't understand what was happening in her life. As a young woman, she felt that she was in control of her destiny. Now she felt like her destiny was a bumper car ride, and she was getting knocked around left and right.

A mother of two kids, 9 and 7, her life was reduced to getting them off to school, working the breakfast-lunch shift at the diner, picking them up, the homework-dinner-bath-bedtime routine, then back to the diner for the nine-to-closing shift. She rarely saw Jerry other than mornings or when she was climbing into bed at night. Some nights she'd come home and he was still up in his office on his laptop, doing Lord knows what.

She still loved Jerry. Always did. The day of her cousin Benny's wedding, she was not looking for a man or a marriage. She was finishing her Associate's degree and thinking about going for a four-year degree in Hospitality Management. Within days of meeting Jerry, all that changed. She fell for him hard, and wanted to be his wife. She saw a life filled with love and children and pets and adventure. All she got was the children.

As a ten-year old when her parent's split up, she was devastated by the divorce. An only child, she was sure she had done something wrong to cause it. Not by being bad; just by not being enough. Maybe if she'd been a better student or a prettier kid. Or nicer to her dad, whom she clashed with often. Maybe then they would have stayed together. As an adult she came to understand that wasn't true. But even if your mind grasps a difficult concept, your inner child holds those early imprints of guilt and shame. She wanted to be a better mother than hers had been, and a better wife. What she was coming to learn is that you can't be a good wife in a vacuum. You need a good partner as well.

Those first few years with Jerry were so loving. Sure, they had their difficult moments, like their wedding day when he made that toast. She was sure her maid of honor would never speak to her again. That vulgar "best woman" joke? Who talks like that about another woman in front of his bride and her parents on their wedding day? Or any day? Her dad wanted to punch him. Not the best way to start a marriage.

She knew that in some way she had pressured Jerry into a covenant wedding. She was always more spiritual than him, even though he'd been going to church with her a lot. She knew in her heart he was never going to be a man of faith. But she had hoped he'd at least be a man of substance. She thought demanding a covenant commitment would make her a better person. What it made her was a better victim.

Things started out well, Leslie would tell herself. *Jerry was working so hard in those days. When he lost his programming job at Ross-Woody, he pounded the pavement until he landed his current job selling cyber software. And aside from Nashville, he had been a great provider. That woman was such a See-You-Next-Tuesday. Like Jerry would ever knowingly email porn links to a female associate. If he said he was hacked, he was hacked. These things happen. Even to a cybersecurity expert. There was no reason to bring the police into it. And certainly no reason to file a sexual harassment complaint. Gold diggers come in all shapes and sizes,* Leslie thought. *And that woman was clearly out for her pot of gold.*

After the two-month suspension (without pay, no less!) Jerry doubled down on his work ethic and made salesman of the month three times in three years. Oh sure, you could say that's not a great track record for a company with only four sales people. But Jerry's specialty is service, not sales. He's never been a people person. He's better with hardware and software.

Maybe that's why he seems so distant with the kids, Leslie wondered as she shifted on her pillow. *If you're not a people person, you're probably not a kid person, either. I know Jerry loves them. He just shows it differently than other fathers. And as far as the birthdays problem, he never had a good memory for anything. Hell, he can hardly remember our anniversary or my birthday. It's no wonder he has trouble remembering the kids' birthdays. He wasn't even there when Megan was born. Working so hard on the road those last five months of my pregnancy. And so hard the two years following. He barely got to see them. Or me. He must've been so lonely! I was lonely and I had the kids to keep me company.*

Yes, Leslie was in massive denial. Where other people saw a slob and a cad, she saw a man who meant well but maybe lost his moral compass now and then. That's why she wanted a covenant marriage. To make sure his "impulses" didn't get the better of him when he would get mad at her during their courtship and disappear for a day or weekend at a time. But he never raised a hand to her or cheated on her, that she knew. Which is why she was always going to stick in there with him.

I mean, sure, maybe I could do better. You always see guys on the street or in the casino diner and think they'd be nicer, warmer, more passionate, more...everything. But those guys are just a mirage. I picked Jerry and he picked me. That's REAL. Just because your marriage isn't perfect, you don't got chasing a dream. Mom and Dad gave up so quickly, and look where that got them. Okay, I suppose Wes is a good man and he treats her well. And earns a lot more than Dad ever did, no doubt about that. But she had to kiss a lot of frogs to find a Wes. And Dad never did settle down with another woman. I don't want that to be me. I don't wanna spend the rest of my thirties, forties and fifties kissing frogs. I met my prince. Sure, he's not a perfect Disney prince. But he's the man I love and the man I chose. If I chose wrong, that's on me, not him. Heck, maybe the problems between us are my fault, too. I should've gotten my B.A. and had a real career. Like all those business women he works with and has those great, interesting phone conversations with.

*All he can talk about with me is what the Daily
Special was. If anything, I'm not good enough for
HIM. Jerry deserved better.*

Her thoughts were interrupted by the creek of
the bedroom doorknob.

"There you are," she said as Jerry entered the
darkened room. "What are you doing up so late?"

"Just finishing up some paperwork." Jerry
crossed into the bathroom for a goodnight pee.

"You work so hard, hon," she called to him.
No response.

In a beat, Jerry came out, leaving the
bathroom light on, and started to get into bed.

"Could you turn out the light?"

"What if I have to pee again?"

"That's what the nightlight is for."

"I can't see shit with that thing."

"Jerry. I have to be up at—"

"Okay, okay!" Jerry got up and grudgingly
turned off the bathroom light. As he got back into
bed...

"Happy?"

Leslie thought about it. Then silently cried
herself to sleep.

❖ ❖ ❖ ❖ ❖

At the bar, Ken saw three women whom he knew to be hookers. One was a former NBC sitcom star whose fame had lasted about as long as a two-dollar umbrella. Now she was turning tricks and making more than she did in her TV days. The others were just great looking women who were paying down the plastic surgery bills.

Sky Bar is what the name implies, a drinking hole at the top of the Mondrian Hotel on the Sunset Strip, an adult tree-house for the SASA crowd ("Super Attractive, Sexually Active"). Ken didn't really fit in there; he was only "nice looking." But then again, he wasn't there for the sport. He was there on business. Just like the hookers.

"Feldie!" Ian grinned from under a white Fedora. The four girls at the table weren't as pleased to see Ken.

"I-man. You don't look like a weeping, love-sick puppy to me."

Ian took off his hat and held it dangling off the table above his lap. "Shit. I haven't been dick-sick since I was eleven. And it didn't last long." Ian winced – subtly, but Ken noticed – and Ken wasn't sure whether it was an involuntary tick or something more serious.

"You see the brunette at the bar?" Ken tossed

his head to indicate.

"I got eyes."

"You know what that is? That's prime-time tang."

"Yeah, at five Gs a pop." Ian scoffed. "Not worth it, believe me."

"Are any of them?"

"Ohh, yeah. I've had some that were worth five big. I didn't pay for them, mind you. But I woulda if I had to. Gladly." Ian grimaced again. Ken tried not to acknowledge it. Ian's pain was not what he was after.

"Whaddaya drinking," Ken asked as he pulled up an empty chair.

"I'm set. So, what did you wanna know?"

"What everybody wants to know. The truth about you and Myra." The girls at the table frowned. That's not what they came to Sky Bar to discuss.

"The truth? That what you gonna print?"

"I only embellish if you don't." That was Ken's rule. *Make what you give me interesting or I will.*

Ian chuckled. "Okay, here's the God's honest truth. No embellishment necessary."

Ken reflexively leaned forward.

"Myra and me, we were cool for a while. Great girl – great body – fun. No, that's bullshit. I loved her. No down in that." Ian liked to pepper his dialog with some kind of white guy's street lingo that Ken couldn't quite place as having any common lineage. It was simply the affectation of a young mega-star who'd never had the time to develop a real personality.

"No down in that," Ken echoed.

"I was planning to go the whole nine. The ring, the priest, the big shindig. Just like she had with Derek. But she got too clingy. Too jealous and shit. Called me one night when I was with someone else and went ballistic, as if I was her boyfriend or something. And frankly, married or not, being faithful to one piece of tail just ain't in the cards for this gunslinger." Ian slumped slightly in his seat, then looked up with a big grin. "But the headline is, between the sheets, it was already sliding."

"Really?!" Ken's eyes widened. "Because shit, man, I could never walk away from a body like that."

"No, she is spectacular. I give her that. Great parts. But that's not the sum total of what gets me off. It's a performance, man. You know that. Moves…attitude…creativity. No, we had laughs, man. Don't get me wrong. Great gal. But she lost me there those last few weeks."

"Between the sheets?" Ken repeated it for the quote. Ian nodded.

"Yup. Shit, Kenny, I think I'll take that drink. Whiskey. Any. Be a bud and do the run?"

The look on Ian's face said it was more than a whim; he needed something. Ken didn't want to find out what was wrong, so he got up to do the movie star's bidding.

At the bar, the sitcom honey-turned-hooker was making time with the lead packaging agent at CAA. *Hmm,* Ken thought, *wonder which of her careers they're talking about.* The bartender was also engrossed in an intense conversation with a blonde who seemed to be reaching across the bar with her breasts. Ken tried to get his attention and eventually did – but that didn't mean his service was forthcoming. A tip is a tip, but a 42-inch bust is a deal breaker. No matter, within seconds a waitress who could be a Victoria's Secret model asked Kenny if she could get him something.

"Two Johnnie Walker Blacks and one phone number. Yours."

She wasn't amused.

"Two Walker Blacks. Tab?"

Ken dropped a fifty on her tray. "What about the phone number?"

She glanced at the cash. "That won't even buy you the area code."

She moved off. Ken turned back to Ian's table and almost did a double-take as a girl in a white dress seemed to rise up from nowhere into the empty seat beside him. *Five girls? Was she there a second ago? Were there five girls there before or four.* Ken watched, bemused, as the mystery girl wiped her mouth on a napkin and began to apply fresh lipstick. Meanwhile, Ian straightened up in his chair, caught Ken's eye and grinned from ear to ear. Ken replayed the grimacing "tick" in his mind. *Holy shit*, he marveled to himself. *I just interviewed a guy while he was getting a blow job!* Ian was too cool, Ken thought. Getting head while talking about your break-up? Too fucking cool.

The waitress returned with two Johnnie Walkers. And eight dollars change.

"Where's the rest of it?"

She raised her eyebrows and sighed. "Guess this is the end of our love affair, huh?" She seemed amused at her own wit.

"Nope" Ken said, picking up seven dollars and leaving just one. "*This* is the end."

She started to walk away. "Oh," Ken bellowed. She turned back to him. "Could I get fifty cents change? In case the price on that phone number comes down overnight."

She dropped the buck at his feet and walked off to resume her life.

◆ ◆ ◆ ◆ ◆

Leslie Proud came down the Berber stairs buttoning the skirt of her waitress uniform. At the bottom, she was surprised to see Jerry already at the breakfast table, reading the paper. It wasn't like him to be up when she left for work. "Hi." She was genuinely pleased.

"Morning," he said with a sip of coffee.

"Why are you up so early?"

Jerry shrugged. "We haven't had a pleasant morning together in a while." Jerry got up to refresh the coffee in his chipped Pittsburgh Steelers mug. "Wanna cup?"

"Thanks," she said as he grabbed her an MTV mug and poured. Leslie wasn't used to somebody serving her for a change. She took the mug from his hand and sipped. "Mmm." Jerry didn't do a lot of things great, but he knew how to make good coffee.

"Kids awake?"

"Megan's getting dressed. Luke is still in bed."

They smiled conspiratorially. Luke asleep equaled blissful quiet. She slid next to him, leaning back against the counter. There they stood, side by side, silently sipping.

"You going in today?"

"Nah. Just making some calls. I may have to do a trip next week. Depends on the Hewlett-Packard deal."

Leslie stroked his hair. "You work so hard." Jerry nodded; they both knew that wasn't true. Leslie just liked to play him…to keep him calm. "I got you something yesterday."

"Another shirt?"

Leslie smiled. "I know the rules. I didn't spend anything." She reached into her bag, pulled out some kind of printed catalogue, and held it up.

"*Dinnertime University*? What's that for?"

"I thought you might wanna, y'know, take

some classes…explore some topics that interest you."

Jerry leafed through it, scoffing. "Why me?"

"You need a hobby. Something to get your mind off things."

"Classes?"

"You loved your electives in college. This whole school is electives! Look. 'Tai Chi'…'Fly Fishing for Beginners'…" She flipped to the page she'd earmarked and whispered. "Tantra Sex and The Endless Orgasm…?" She meant it as joke between lovers, but he took it as a putdown.

"You trying to tell me something?"

"Come on, I'm kidding." Leslie's voice pleaded lovingly. "You're so, I don't know… distracted lately. You need some fun. Just flip through it today. I'll bet there's something in there that'll appeal to you."

"MOM!" That voice could split an atom. "WHAT'D YOU DO WITH MY CAMOUFLAGE SNEAKERS?!"

Luke was up. The peaceful morning was over.

The following week, Leslie finished her Tuesday shift early, since it was one-twelve and the casino dinner was empty. On the way home, she stopped at the Walmart for some groceries and new pants for Luke. Luke outgrew pants faster than they faded. On the checkout line, Leslie couldn't help but notice the headline. "Ian to Myra: 'You lost me between the sheets.'" She flipped to the article and smirked at the details. *How could one woman make so many bad choices?*

Four dollars and thirty five cents later, *The American Peephole* was in a bag, nestled between the Maxwell House coffee and three pairs of Levis that would barely last Luke four months.

Chapter 4

*I*n prosecutor parlance, it was a "bad murder." Of course, to the civilized world, all murder is bad. But when you deal with murder every day, when it is not an abstract concept but a daily, tangible fact of life, you use mental defense mechanisms to cope with it. One way is with a morbid, graveyard sense of humor, and most of the prosecutors in the Fulton County D.A.'s office had that. But the other way to deal with murder is to subdivide it into genres. Mental files to distinguish the robbery homicide from the gang-banger shootout to the domestic abuse gone too far.

Even in the category of atrocities, there were subcategories that allowed the Assistant District Attorneys to compartmentalize human horror into definable concepts. Sure, he was stabbed 27 times, but he probably went into shock after the first artery was cut and passed out long before the final wounds were inflicted. Yes, it must have been terrifying to have a plastic dry cleaners bag duct taped around your head at the neck. But her efforts to gasp for air probably obscured the fact that an electric nail gun was being pointed at her temple, and the jolt of the nail probably numbed the victim to the seven more that would perforate her brain.

But Amy Clousterman fell into that special category of murders the Assistant D.A.s reserved for those deaths that even made hardened veterans weep. Amy Clousterman was only eighteen, a first year student at Emory University. Amy had moved to the Atlanta campus from Utica, New York, a relatively small town, and she never quite got the hang of city life. Feeling lonely and disconnected from her classmates and roommate, Amy frequented bars on light study nights and was not immune from finding social acceptance in the bed of a strange man. The last man she would look to for a fix of affection and understanding was Trey Pruitt Scott. What she got was something very different.

"What does a girl have to do to get a drink around here?

The bartender snickered. "Turn twenty-one."

"I have ID." Amy waved her fake New York driver's license.

"And I'm Santa Claus." The bartender disappeared down the bar.

That's when Trey Scott made his move.

"Seems you're shit outta luck."

Amy glanced his way and sized him up. "Only in this shit hole."

"Is that what college girls do for fun these days? Bounce from dive to dive trying to buy a beer?"

"I don't drink beer. Mixed drinks only."

"Ah, a woman of refined tastes." He held out his hand. "Trey."

"Amy." She shook it tentatively.

"Hi Amy. Well, he already busted you as underage. Otherwise I'd step up and buy a round for you. But I hate to see you have to hop from bar to bar in this rain just to get a Cosmopolitan."

"And you suggest…?"

"I buy us the spirits of your choice and we share a toast at my place."

"I don't know you."

"Yet." Trey smiled. "Hence the invitation."

She thought he was cute. And he was right about the rain.

"My place. My roommate's out of town. I'll feel safer there."

"I think I'm a tad offended by that." Trey smiled just enough to show he was kidding.

Amy moved closer. "Then let's say, I'll feel less inhibited. Trey." She touched her hand to his chest.

"Your place it is."

They walked the two blocks to a liquor store huddled under his umbrella, settled on a bottle of Kraken Rum, then hailed a cab for the eight block trip back to her apartment. After one block, Trey had his hand on her thigh. By the end of the third block, they were kissing. By the time the cabbie stopped in front of her building, Trey had already penetrated her with his fingers.

Trey thanked the driver, grabbed the paper bag holding their nightcap, and helped her out his door. Amy found her keys in her purse and ushered him inside.

Two flights up, they were in her very modest loft. The two minute tour took all of eight seconds.

73

"Cute place." Trey noticed all the girly appointments, like the non-working pink princess phone perched on the end table for decorative effect.

"That's where I sleep. Trina sleeps upstairs." End of tour.

"Glasses?"

"Over the microwave."

Trey had barely grabbed two glasses and unscrewed the bottle when Amy started to undress.

◆ ◆ ◆ ◆ ◆

Trey Scott was a ladies' man, for sure, so it was no surprise he was able to literally charm Amy's pants off. Not that Amy was all that picky. But she was very definitive about her likes and dislikes in the sex arena. Amy loved intercourse, and by the time Trey had undone her bra she had already decided on at least three positions she would fuck him in. Amy loved being on top, and that was always first in her compendium. She loved to take a man in her hands and bring him to her, guiding, placing, and ultimately deciding the moment she would let him feel his prize. But she also enjoyed doggie style and the exquisite shock of being entered from behind. And tonight, being in a particularly lonely frame of mind, she needed at least a few moments of missionary, where she could look into Trey's narrow, steel blue eyes and project the warm, sincere affection and even – yes, even the love that she always felt for a man and needed to feel in return.

Trey, on the other hand, had a more robust sexual experience in mind. He didn't mind screwing a girl this way and that, but he liked other things too, including getting some good head. For that matter, any head, because for Trey, there was no bad head. Sure, it felt good to be inside a girl, especially the petite ones like Amy, who tended to be tight. It always made Trey feel bigger, more powerful, when he felt something pushing back against his cock. But the best sensation, the feeling Trey thought about when he thought about sex, was the indescribable feeling of fellatio. For pure pleasure, there was nothing - nothing! - that felt like moistened lips slithering down your shaft. And for that, of course, you needed head. Not the fast, pounding, sloppy lip head that most women gave. That was okay. But Trey really got hard when it was slow and teasing, with her teeth lightly scratching, a combination that was highly gratifying and, well, just a wee bit painful. He figured it had something to do with how he was initiated to sexual pleasure. From as early as he could remember, his preferred method of masturbation was face down, rubbing the bottom of his erection against the bed sheet or blanket or, for variety, on denim jeans or carpeting. It simulated the missionary position, especially with a pillow to caress. But it was the sensation of rubbing, the dry friction against rough surfaces, that he came to associate with great pleasure. And to this day, no vagina could ever match that feeling of course, sharp scratching. Some men get hot eyeing boobs or legs or lips. Trey was turned on by teeth.

Amy didn't like head. Not giving; not receiving. She knew some girls were turned on by it, some even liked giving better than receiving. But Amy found it, well, there's no other word: dirty. It was not sensual or satisfying to her. It was an ordeal, an icky, messy ordeal that never tasted good and frankly struck her as gross. *I wouldn't swallow snot. Or puss. Or anything else that oozes, drips, spews or seeps. Why would I want to ingest that?!* she'd reason to herself, blanching at the thought.

So when Trey gently tried to guide her down

to his crotch, she pushed away. "Come on, just a little, baby. I need you," he instructed.

"No. There's so much *else* I want to do to you," she purred back.

"There ain't nothing else. Please." His hand pushed down harder.

"No, baby. I want you inside me." She meant it.

"Hey, I wanna be inside you, too. In your mouth. Now come on."

He grabbed some hair and pulled her face back into him. She shook her head and pried herself away.

Trey had had enough. He rolled onto her and wedged himself between her lips. At first she resisted with a clinched jaw, until she could almost feel her teeth coming loose from her gums. When she parted them a crack, he pushed in. Soon he was fucking her in the mouth.

Amy fought and wriggled, refusing to allow him to rape her this way. The pressure of the sharp cutting edges of her fangs only made Trey want more. His skin was being ripped, but surprisingly, it didn't hurt. He liked it. No. He loved it!

Amy tasted his salty blood and began to cry. This loosened her jaw just enough for Trey to make full penetration. Soon his spastic movements flowed into full, deep thrusts. Amy struggled to breathe. Trey pounded harder, harder until she could see him arch back. Then her mouth flooded. A wet, thick, bitter eruption that made her gag and cough. Amy turned on her side and spit out what she could, frantically rubbing her tongue clean on her sheets.

"You fuckin' bastard!"

"You loved it," he said as he wiped himself dry on her blanket.

"YOU FUCKING BASTARD!"

"Hey, keep your voice down. Let's not spoil a good time."

"You think that's what this was? You think this was a good time?!" Amy's face was red and wet and spotted with blood.

Trey nonchalantly pulled on his Calvins. "What would you call it?"

"Rape. I'd call it rape."

"Oh, please," he dismissed her with a grin.

"You think it's funny? You think I'm

kidding?" She reached for her cellphone. "You fucking bastard!"

"What are you doing?"

"I'm calling the police, that's what I'm – "

Trey ripped the cellphone from her hand. Amy slapped him and he slapped her back, hard. "Gimme that!" As Amy tried to wrestle the cellphone back, she never saw the pink princess phone handset in his other hand, hurtling through space toward her temple. The blow knocked her onto the bed and tumbling over it. Trey knew he was no longer on a date.

"God damn you!" Still dizzy, she touched the bruise. "I will see you rot behind bars, you son of a bitch." Amy still thought she had some power left, some leverage that made this a two-sided argument. But it had ceased to be a quarrel between two people with any level of give and take. It was now one God-like being totally dominating his universe and everything that was in it, including Amy. She tried to get up. Trey pushed her back down.

"Get the fuck out of here!!"

"Oh, I plan to," Trey said coldly, pulling his belt from around his waist. "In due time."

With that, the belt was around her neck. Amy struggled briefly, but even the few scratches she could make in Trey's face and arms were a mist in the path of a tidal wave. He pulled her backwards by her neck, backing her into a chair, then ripped a chord from the curtains and used it to tie her in. Trey looked around the room. No rope. No other belts. But on the desk, next to her laptop – Trey grabbed the Scotch tape dispenser.

Is he gonna hit me with it? Cut me with it? Amy had no idea. She could not conceive that his approach was so much more reasoned. He bound her with it.

And to both her amazement and the pleasant surprise of Trey, numerous passes of the cellophane tape around her torso held her in place. You wouldn't think that something so easy to break in one layer could be so impressively strong in eight or ten layers. But it was. Amy was immobilized.

Trey picked up Amy's black panties and sniffed them sweetly.

"We got a problem here, baby. And I only see one solution." Trey scrunched up the panties in his right hand and rummaged through her desk with his left.

"I'm sorry," she whimpered. "I was a bitch. I am always such a bitch."

"You said a mouth full." He chuckled. "First you got a mouthful, then you said a mouthful." Trey chuckled as he scrounged in the drawer until his hand came out holding a long, thin pair of scissors.

"No, really. I'm sorry. I really am. Just go and leave me be and I promise–"

Trey shoved the panties between her teeth. "That's the thing with promises made under duress. The person always means it at the time. But I can't take a chance of you changing your mind."

Amy spit out enough of the black satin to be able to speak.

"You don't want to kill me."

"Never said I *wanted* to, honey." Trey fingered the scissor blades for sharpness.

"People saw us," she countered. "There are witnesses. The bar."

"They won't remember us." Trey smiled.

"You don't know that. And my building. My building has video cameras. At the front door. When we came in."

Trey was slowly moving toward her. "It was pretty dark."

"This is insane! Your DNA is all over this place. They'll find your semen on the bed. They'll find it in *me*!"

"Yeah. But they ain't gonna find me to match it to." Trey moved even closer.

"I'll scream!"

"Yes, you will." She began a scream, but Trey shoved the panties deep into her mouth, muffling it. Then pulled the Scotch tape around her head. Amy screamed and screamed. All that she heard coming out was muted groans.

"I did this to a boy once. Unlike you, he *knew* how to give head." Trey edged the scissor against her ear. "Then he told me he had AIDS. Fuckin' asshole. So I took a Philips screwdriver…" Trey tickled the scissor blade next to her ear. "…and went digging."

Amy was a basket case by now. Crying, wiggling, pleading, whimpering.

"You know why? I mean, of course, you know why I killed him. But d' ya know why I did it *that* way?"

Amy shook her head, whimpering more.

"No blood. Oh sure, there was some that trickled out. Especially after the third or fourth thrust." She cried harder. "But, see, if you stab somebody from the front or the back, there's gonna be blood shootin' all over, and there's no way to keep it from getting on you. This way, the bleeding is almost all internal. In the skull. Much easier to control." He smiled. "Bet you're wishing you had shut up and blown me now."

Amy could only nod and cry.

Trey grabbed a pillow from the bed and shook off the pillow case. "Know what the papers said? When they found him and did the autopsy, know what? They said he might not have died from the holes in his brain. He might've been alive for one or two hours after. I was sure from his eyes he wasn't, but what do I know. I'm no doctor. They said the blood slowly swelled in his cranium 'til his brain kinda just collapsed in under the pressure. What do you think that feels like, when your brain gets slowly squashed? You have no idea, do you?" He paused for effect. "But you're gonna find out…"

Amy screamed and struggled one last time.

"'Course, his wounds were probably cleaner, seein' how a screwdriver is so much more precise than a scissor blade. With a screwdriver I could twist and probe 'til the Phillips head found just the right spot. You know the spot when their eyes start to turn weird circles in their sockets. It'll be hard to get that same precision with a wedge-shaped blade." Amy pleaded with her wet eyes. It meant nothing to Trey. "All I can do," he tossed his head casually, "is try."

Trey balled up the pillow case in his left hand and gently cradled it under her ear.

In the mirror over the dressing table, Amy saw the point of the blade peeking into her ear and felt the sting of cut skin. Then watched it moving further…disappearing…into her head, like a magician swallowing a sword.

Amy felt the metal rushing into her ear canal. Then pain! The sharpest, loudest pain imaginable – her eardrum bursting. Inside her head, the movement felt like an itch. Amy knew that the brain had no nerve endings, no feeling. She'd learned that in Intro to Physiognomy. But she could *feel* it. Moving. Tickling. He head and eyes rolled spasmodically as Trey probed insider her.

Then the bloody scissor blade was in front of her eyes as Trey wiped it off. Amy saw the grey gook from the blade sticking to the pillow case and knew she was dying.

Trey smiled, pursed his lips and blew her a kiss. Then moved in for another pass.

Trey was picked up by the police two days later after a tip from the cab driver. Not the smartest man in the world, Trey had forgotten that he paid for the ride to her building with his credit card. His fingerprints were lifted from the cab and the apartment. And yes, his DNA was found on her sheets and in her abdomen.

A jury wasted little time finding Trey Pruitt Scott guilty of first-degree murder. His police confession, coupled with the premeditated nature of the crime, made it pretty much a slam dunk for the State. "First Degree Homicide with Exceptional Depravity" was the official charge, but even that seemed somehow inadequate to describe the deed. During the sentencing phase of the trial, the prosecutor used the slang term "bad murder" to communicate to the judge and jury why Trey Scott deserved a sentence of death and no less.

"We have a term in the Homicide unit of the D.A.'s office," Assistant D.A. Beth Sherman argued during the sentencing phase. "A term we save for the most heinous crimes men commit against men. We call it 'bad murder.'" Beth moved out from behind her podium to make her point. "Isn't that redundant? *Bad* murder? No. Because we believe that even in death, even in violent, premeditated deaths caused by one person against another, a living being deserves certain fundamental human rights. And at the top of those rights is the right not to know you are about to die." Beth stared down the jury box. "In a robbery, in a shooting, in a murder of rage, even in those horrific instances, the intended victim still has a hope – "a fighting chance," we like to call it – a prayer of hope that they may survive the awful attack. But when you are taped and bound into a chair…when you are told you are about to be executed, as Amy Clousterman was…when you see the scissor blade going into your skull…see it in the mirror…feel it piercing your eardrum and surging deeper into your head. Feeling your cerebral cortex being sliced and scraped out from within. Seeing bits of your brain oozing out of your ear and onto your lap. As parts of your body begin to shut down.

First speech. Then fingers and limbs. Nerve endings. Eyesight. Your body spasms uncontrollably. Yet you're still mentally aware. And you know – you KNOW – that you are dying." She paused for effect. "When you are forced to experience the terror of seeing your life come to an end, not in a quick spasm of violence but in a slow ballet of grotesque horror. Neither the police, nor the District Attorneys...not even the coroners or the pathologists...none of the professionals who deal with murder every single day can fathom what Amy Clousterman must have experienced, the inhuman cruelty of feeling her brain being sliced apart inside her head and knowing she was dying."

Beth took a calculated breath. "It wasn't just murder. It was exceptional depravity. It was bad murder."

The jury agreed.

In the fourteen years Trey Scott was on death row, his attorneys tried every type of appeal. But it wasn't until they reached the Ninth Circuit Court of Appeals that defense lawyer Robert F. Lowenstein tried the Hail Mary of all legal arguments. "The sentence of death, to be prescribed and imposed at a precise time in a precise manner, is no different than the crime the state of Georgia says my client imposed on his victim," Lowenstein calmly told the Court. "In her own presentation to the trial court during sentencing, Assistant District Attorney Elizabeth Sherman argued that the fact the victim knew the precise moment and method of her death was so cruel... exhibited such exceptional depravity...as to be inhuman in nature. By that same logic, is it not depraved and inhumane for the state to end Trey Scott's life in the same manner?"

It was an argument that every other lawyer on Scott's defense team had dismissed as ludicrous.

It was the argument the Ninth Circuit used to overturn the sentence.

Among the law clerks who worked in the United States Supreme Court, there was a shorthand they used to ridicule each others' bosses. Supreme Court clerks are an intellectually snobbish bunch by nature, and generally see themselves as mentally superior to the doddering geezers for whom they research, write and think. But even in whispered conversations, no clerk would dare disparage another clerk's Justice by name. The nicknames they used, which only they and they alone knew, were a right of egalitarian passage, a verbal secret handshake.

While not particularly as elegant as those of previous Courts, the names for the current crop of justices were no less demeaning. "The Chief Jewstice" was branded by the rabbinical career he held before his appointment to the Court as well as the annoyingly theological views he brought to his written opinions.

Of the two women on the Court, "The Schoolmarm" was the most admired, tarred in nickname only by her trademark granny glasses and reddish-gray hair that was always pulled back in a tight bun. One former Jewstice clerk had pitched that she be known as "Granny," but that was chucked in respect after her teenaged granddaughter committed suicide. At the other end of the political spectrum was the universally disrespected "Madam Justits," who most of the clerks (and the law community in general) believed was more modestly endowed in the cranial area than in her ample chest region, which had its own nickname, "the thirteenth circuit." (There are only twelve federal circuit courts in the United States.)

"Justice Wiener" was not nicknamed for his appendage or personality, but for his oft-stated admiration for Felix Frankfurter, the legendary Justice after whom he had modeled his career and whom he would cite in almost every major dissent. It was also the only name that took into account the Justice's real name, as his first name, Oscar, is shared by the food company that makes the world's most famous wiener. And the contrast between the legendary Justice Frankfurter and the all-too-forgettable Justice Weiner are as obvious as the differences between that other odd couple, Oscar and Felix, an irony not lost on the other clerks.

"Judge Dred" earned his name somewhat for his lineage in civil rights litigation (hence, Dred Scott) but mostly for his irrational fear of appearing in public, which kept him from making personal appearances of any kind. Even on the day of his nomination to the Court, Judge Dred begged out on the presidential announcement ceremony, citing a "previous commitment."

The youngest of the nine justices, "The Benchwarmer" was assumed to have won his name because he virtually never speaks in open court, often giving the impression that he was the Supreme

Court's first "alternate" judge, waiting patiently to be put in the game. But in reality, his nickname assumes that he was named by the sitting president for purely political reasons, he not having the votes in Congress to get his first five choices passed. The inside line on the Benchwarmer is that he will retire early in the second term, the pre-determined pretense being "health reasons" due to his well-known battle with coronary disease, to be replaced by a real neoconservative more to the president's liking.

Then there were the other, purely descriptive character assassinations. The weak-bladdered "Whizz Honor" earned his term of endearment for his inability to get through an oral argument without availing himself of the ceremonial spittoons that had sat with dignity under the bench for two hundred years before being unceremoniously tapped for this duty. "The Godfather" had the coolest nickname, thanks to his Italian ancestry and Brando-esque scowl. But maybe the most original was "The Justice of the Piece," ridiculed for his well-known penchant to wear a Colt .45 under his robe, though another version combines his ethnicity and ultra-right winged views on crime into the all encompassing, "Marshal Thurgood."

While the oral arguments for Georgia versus Scott were unremarkable, the closed-door deliberations were highly contentious. It started with a basic recounting of the facts by the Chief Jewstice. Then his associates began their considered analysis of case at hand. It was the Judge Dred who first seemed to warm to the Lowenstein argument to overturn the sentence.

"I must say, he brought the Fourteenth under a whole new set of lights. What's good for the goose…"

"Bullshit," mumbled The Justice of the Piece, using colloquial plain talk as he often did to punctuate his points. "It's just another attempt to reinterpret the amendment. There was nothing original in Scott's position. Everything is cruel and unusual when it's happening to *you*. He wasn't thinking about cruelty or normalcy when he was torturing another person. Then he's facing the gas chamber and all of a sudden the asshole has a constitutional epiphany?"

"We'll limit the scope of our deliberations to the issues and arguments," the Chief Jewstice interjected, "…and with civility." He knew his black brethren could adopt a colorful vernacular when his hang-'em-high world view was under attack, and the Chief didn't want to see this deliberation turn ugly.

The Schoolmarm pushed her glasses up her nose, as she often did to demonstrate her distaste for profanity. "I was more intrigued by the concept of 'equitable process.' This Court has erred on the side of due process for over one and a half centuries. Frankly, I'm not sure to the best results."

"I am." The Godfather was nothing if not concise in his arguments.

"And you have no reservations about the hypocrisy of executing a man for the crime of executing a woman?"

"It's called an eye for an eye," came the Godfather's rejoinder.

The Benchwarmer nodded twice. Fairly demonstrative by his standards.

"That's a common law argument," said Whizz Honor, crossing his legs, "not a constitutional one."

Madam Justits dove into the fray. "The constitution is a common law document."

The Schoolmarm had come to expect community college reasoning from her buxom associate, yet was stupefied by that baseless comment. "Since when?"

"Well, common law in the sense that it was drafted to reflect common sense and morality."

"At that time." Judge Dred had no stomach for blind adherence to strict constitutionalism.

The Justice of the Piece was angling for a shootout. "There was nothing 'common' about equal protection under the law. What set the document apart at its time was the originality of its world view."

Whizz Honor pinched his legs together and squirmed in his seat. "I'm bothered by this 'eye for an eye' rationale. I think we do a disservice to the plaintiff by considering biblical law in a constitutional matter."

The Schoolmarm was playing to the swing votes. "I'm not saying that the due process argument is without merit. I'm just not sure that in Trey Scott we have chosen the best line in the sand."

"Amy Clousterman might beg to differ. Just

as she begged for her life." The Godfather would have none of her bleeding-heart liberalism on a death penalty case.

"We're not passing judgment on Trey Scott. The state of Georgia has already done that." The Chief Jewstice was trying to avoid showing his hand, in case a split was in the offing. "But there is something to be said for re-examining certain issues in light of new thinking. Conventional wisdom is not an argument of law."

"It is when it aligns with precedent," countered Justice Wiener.

"This case is not a matter of conventional wisdom," Judge Dred protested. "Forgive me, but we are an interpretive body. A man has asked us to interpret the Fourteenth amendment based on a set of facts. The facts are what is new here."

"There's nothing 'new' about the death penalty," Madam Justits said, showing her penchant for stating the obvious.

"No, but there is everything new about a state that has redefined their application." Judge Dred was on a roll. "'Cruel and unusual' is in the eye of the beholder."

"*We* are the beholder." The Godfather seemed defensive.

"I am sorry, Mr. Justice, but you are wrong," the Whizz Honor fired back, squeezing his thighs together tightly. "We are the judicial function of the federal government. The state is the one in this case that is empowered to prescribe death. They define a standard and we determine if they have met it objectively."

"And they have!" The Justice of the Piece was also running nervous. "Aggravated homicide with extreme depravity."

"With all due respect…" The Benchwarmer speaks?! All eyes turned to him. "…not when the state revises its own legal definition of 'extreme depravity' to include telling someone they are going to die and then killing them. If Georgia thinks it is 'depraved' to give a victim specific notice of her imminent death, they should abide by those same rules. It's a basic principal of parity."

"Parity?" The Chief Jewstice seemed baffled.

The Benchwarmer continued authoritatively. "With Cruzan and Glucksberg, this court used constitutionally protected rights to preserve life. I see no reason to ignore stare decisis in this matter. We have previously recognized all sorts of right to life issues, right to death issues, privacy, conflicting interests. Maybe it's time to establish a clear, proactive right."

"And what right would that be?"

"The right to die naturally. I.e., without prior notice. In other words, a good death."

The brief silence bespoke the admiration of his fellow brethren. While the clerks often mistook The Benchwarmer's silence for a lack of original thought, those inside the chamber knew otherwise. Before and during oral arguments, it had been assumed the Benchwarmer would vote with the conservative block. But here he was showing his ability to go his own way and defy conventional thinking.

"So you're saying that life itself is not the fundamental human right?" The Chief was intrigued.

The Schoolmarm jumped in. "No one has a right to live forever. Nature makes that impossible. Maybe the issue isn't life or death at all. But rather, advanced knowledge of the time and place of death.

This body has found that active euthanasia violates the state's interests in preserving life, while passive euthanasia is acceptable in some cases. That's a paradox in some minds, but not in law. Maybe the state's interests are equally protected in this case, but the application is faulty."

"I think I see where the Associate Justice is going here," Judge Dred opined. "If the state of Georgia thinks there's such a thing as a bad death – a 'bad murder' in the prosecutor's parlance – then maybe the alternative is a good death."

This was a novel concept indeed. It seemed as if the anti-death penalty advocates were redefining their objection to capital punishment. It wasn't just the methods that were cruel and unusual. It was the convicted felon's advanced awareness of the intended murder itself. That there is an inherent right not to know the place and moment of your death.

Justice Weiner protested. "The Constitution demands neither logical symmetry nor exhaustion of a principle.' Felix Frankfurter, Ullman v. United States."

"I don't think the state's death penalty law was built on a standard of symmetry, Oscar," the

The Godfather countered.

"Then maybe," the Schoolmarm leaned forward and whispered, "it *should be*."

"Your point eludes me," the Madam Justits dismissed.

"Then it's in the clear majority." The Schoolmarm dismissed back. Her colleagues laughed reflexively.

"There, there. We won't need that." The Chief Jewstice hated to defend another judge, but he also knew there was no love lost between the Schoolmarm and Madam Justits, and it was his job to keep things civil.

"The point, Madam Justice," the Schoolmarm calmly reasoned, "...is that plaintiff builds his case on the presumption the state cannot dispense capital punishment in a manner consistent with the concept of extreme depravity, which was its own chosen standard. Well, if it's now considered "depraved" to tell a man on death row the exact time and manner of his execution, maybe it's time the state considered alternate remedies."

"What 'alternate remedies'? Should the state just send Scott back on the streets and hire a hitman?" The Justice of the Piece's colleagues chuckled at his dripping sarcasm.

"Maybe." The Godfather wasn't joking.

"Preposterous." Oscar Weiner hated slippery slope arguments.

"Maybe it is, maybe it isn't," The Benchwarmer was standing his ground. "But that's not the matter before us. Preordained death in a set place and is. If the state of Georgia considers a preordained death to be 'cruel and unusual,' it has to die by its own sword."

"So you're saying the state has a right to take a life, just not to announce it in advance?" The Chief liked to clarify novel arguments by turning it into a Socratic dialogue, especially when they were philosophical in nature.

"We send soldiers into war knowing they may die," Oscar mused out loud. "We test pharmaceuticals knowing the potential adverse outcomes, often including death. Legislators make policy decisions that pit one life against another. We even put down pets that have attacked human beings."

"The difference is, the dog doesn't know he's

about to be killed." Judge Dred saw the slippery slope ahead and was nudging his colleagues down it.

"Exactly," Wiener continued." "The state does not have clean hands when it comes to decisions of life or death. What it does have is discretion in the manner of death. Maybe *that's* what this case is about."

The room went quiet. A consensus was forming. Even Justice Wiener was coming around. The death penalty in the United States was not being affirmed nor overturned.

It was being reconceived.

When the 6-3 decision to overturn the Trey Pruitt Scott sentence and send it back to the trial court came down, the media went full throttle. Here was the U.S. Supreme Court, the defender of capital punishment over two centuries, reversing on the very "cruel and unusual" argument that had once been abandoned to the junkyard of archaic legal concepts. The Court hadn't given credence to a single "cruel and unusual" appeal in over thirty-eight years. Now a state was being told to revamp

101

its entire concept of execution, and every state that had capital punishment on the books would have to do the same.

Legal scholar after legal scholar dissected the Schoolmarm's majority opinion and the dissenting ones that concurred in part, and virtually every expert came to the same inescapable conclusion: the high court had indeed validated the concept of state executions, they just didn't find any method acceptable in which the convicted murderer knew his exact date, time and method of execution.

The Court's majority thought they were striking at the very heart of the death penalty, since a sentence of death was always set to be in a prescribed time and manner. Indeed, that was part of the language of a capital punishment sentence. The last meal, walking the inmate the last mile, offering a blindfold, a final prayer for redemption – these were all assumed to be inherent in a state execution – living organs of the death penalty that could not be excised from it. But what the Court had inadvertently done was tacitly condone the idea that the state could "execute" a convict by surprise.

"A court-sanctioned hit," was how one defense attorney summed it. "Give a man the electric chair and you're out of bounds. Pump a bullet in the back of the head in the mess hall and you're constitutionally sound."

That wasn't the outcome the majority thought they were voting for. But the law of unintended consequences sometimes even applies to the law.

The Georgia legislature, stung by the decision and the fallout, jumped into action. In a quick series of bills drafted and passed that year, the prescribed "method and moment" in which the Department of Corrections was to carry out a capital punishment sentence was "to be at the absolute discretion of the Department of Corrections, using any and every means the Commissioner sees fit to ensure a swift, effective, and unanticipated execution." Similar laws were being drafted by other state legislatures, but the concept was so jarring that there was serious doubt in the legal community they would withstand judicial review.

In the meantime, Trey Scott was a hero on death row, as death sentence after death sentence in Georgia was being appealed or commuted. Within weeks he was back in the general prison population, enjoying some of the best food and best head he had ever known. Two years went by as his attorneys filed brief after brief in an effort to commute his own sentence down to life with a possibility of parole.

On Valentines' Day, the prison theater showed Trey's favorite movie, "Ghostbusters II," and he was granted a first-row seat. During the second reel, a nine-millimeter bullet fired at close range burst through the back of his skull and ended his life.

As the other prisoners scurried away in shock, the movie stopped and the houselights came up.

In the back row, Amy Clousterman's mother silently squeezed her husband's hand, stood up and exited.

Chapter 5

*M*yra Dreyer hated when people talked about her in front of her as if she wasn't there, or not worth acknowledging. In Hollywood, it happened a lot.

"Myra doesn't want to do any junkets."

"Be reasonable, Jeff. I can't tell Sir Dorian Morris that he has to schlep all over the States promoting a film while his co-star sits by her pool in Silver Lake.

With each exchange, Myra's shoulder-length brown hair played peek-a-boo across her blue eyes as her head skipped from one man to the other, a mere spectator in the ping-pong game that was her career. She knew her role, though her agent always felt compelled to coach her while waiting for a meeting to begin. "Let me do the talking," Galaxy Talent super-agent Jeff Josephs would whisper just as the other party sat down. So there she sat, nursing a glass of Pinot, letting her Barbie doll figure and signature brunette bounce do her talking.

"No junkets." If Jeff had a failing as an agent, it was his single-minded insistence on winning every argument. He was a well-manicured, nasty guy who would go to the men's room and purposely get urine on his own right hand before a meeting so when he shook hands with the other party, he knew he had already pissed on them. Myra often wished she had signed with an agent who was more like her, more conciliatory. Myra didn't want to do the junket, that's true; what with the separation from Derek and her medical issues. The last thing she needed was to do twenty-five cities in nineteen days. But she didn't want to anger a studio over the point.

"Give me eight weekends. That's all I ask." Of course, that wasn't all Ray O'Mally was asking. He never asked for only one thing. He simply divided what he wanted into individual negotiations and made each one a deal breaker. Always with the softening touch, "that's all I ask" or "it's the least you can do" or "for the greater good." Funny how only the things that Ray O'Mally wanted were ever for "the greater good."

"She'll do the talks shows. West coast only."

"No Colbert?!" O'Mally looked stunned.

"What about *SNL?*"

Jeff shook his head.

"*SNL?*" Myra was stunned that she'd even be considered. But the way she said it made Jeff think she didn't know the reference.

"Please, Myra, I've got it under control." Josephs patted her knee in that way that she despised, never breaking eye contact with O'Mally. "It's a very difficult time for her, as you can imagine. We want to support the movie. We're proud of it – of our work…"

When did it become "his" work? Myra thought.

"I always wanted to do *Saturday Night Live.*"

O'Mally's head snapped. Jeff Josephs removed his hand from Myra's knee as if it was a punishment. Myra was back in the room.

"We're looking at dates in February. Colbert, Fallon, all three morning shows." O'Mally knew how to play to an actor's ego. "It's a great way to get your side out. That's what Ariana did after the whole Pete Davidson thing."

Myra nodded. Maybe it was time to get her side out about her infamous breakup.

O'Mally moved in for the kill. "I hear this

new kid on *SNL* does a fabulous 'Derek.' I'm no comedy writer, but certainly – "

"Are we plugging a movie or a divorce?" Nope, Josephs did not like to concede a point.

"I'm not afraid to talk about it," Myra interjected. "Better me than that asshole Feldman from *The Peephole*."

"We'll peg some potential dates." O'Mally was closing. "But we're going to need some flexibility visa vi the junkets. Say, six weekends?"

"Two. And a corporate jet." Josephs did not look happy.

"Two weekends? You can do a little more than that, can't you, Myra? The studio knows how rough things are right now. But this film, your great work — wouldn't Ian shit a stream if you did fifty million the first weekend?"

Yes he would, Myra thought. She added to the idea, "Maybe getting out of the house is the best thing for me now."

Jeff Josephs looked down at his tie and sighed. He knew when to argue and when to negotiate. And when your client folds, it's time to negotiate. "How many cities are we talking about?"

If nothing else, Myra was back in the room.

❖ ❖ ❖ ❖ ❖

As always, lunch was about deals. Who had a deal, who needed a deal, who could make a deal. Myra hated this part of work; she didn't understand why every meeting she and Jeff took together had to be preceded or followed by a meal. That's because she didn't need to be seen with Jeff. But Jeff needed to be seen with her. An agent needs to be seen with his important clients. It continually re-validates them in the town's eye. CPR for the image.

Myra felt unusually awkward in public these days. When she had Ian or Derek to lean on, she always felt accepted and beautiful. But like this, out alone, she felt like a 109-pound zit. And sitting across from Jeff Josephs was that feeling, squared.

"Andy! I got your email! Let's talk." Jeff could make any restaurant conversation sound even shallower than it was. "So, My? You feel okay about what we got out of Ray?"

"I guess. What did we get?"

"'What did we get?' Did you want to do a nineteen day junket tour?"

"No."

"Right. So you're just doing four weekends."

"Of three days each. Plus a travel day on each side. Times four, adds up to twenty."

"Yeah, but broken up. And on a company jet,

not some tiny six seater. And aside from the SNL-Colbert week in New York, you don't have to go past the central time zone."

Myra spun her index finger in the air, signaling "whip-dee-doo." A man in a shiny gray suit caught Jeff's eye.

"Sergio! Did you read it?" Whoever Sergio was, he clearly wanted less to do with Jeff than Jeff wanted of him. "Read it tonight. I'll call tomorrow for your thoughts." Myra smiled. Jeff didn't want Sergio's thoughts. He wanted his money.

The waiter brought their crab salads, which caused the unwanted collateral damage of bringing Jeff's attention back to the table he was at.

"So? Ian. What do you hear?"

"I don't hear anything, Jeff. We're not talking." Myra dug into her salad.

"And Derek? And how's that going?"

Myra shrugged. She sensed there was an agenda. "We've spoken a few times."

"So you two thinking about getting back together? Because…y'know…the thing with Ian was out there."

"I seem to recall." Myra sucked a crab leg.

"I'm just saying, if you and Derek are getting serious again, that's great. But let's not forget, we have p.r. issues to balance."

"So what, we shouldn't reconcile?"

"Just the opposite! I *love* that you guys might get back together. I just think you want to do it right this time."

"Okay."

"You know what a covenant marriage is, right?"

"I read about 'em." A pause, as Jeff waited for the idea to register. Myra chuckled. "Oh, you have to be kidding."

"I ran it around the office this morning. Everybody loves it."

"I don't love it."

"Why not?"

"For one thing, we're not religious."

"It's not about religion. It's about commitment. It's about *love.*"

"I don't see how it's anyone's business." Myra snapped a crab leg to punctuate her point.

"Of course, it's no one's business. But then you have assholes like that Ken Feldman at *The Peephole* who make it their business. They make it a fucking industry."

"Can we do something about that son of a bitch?"

"Yes!" Jeff leaned in for emphasis. "That's what I'm talking about. The press, the tabloids, they're eating you alive. 'Leaving one guy for his best friend. Leaving *that guy* to go back with the first guy...' You know how you turn it around for you? You do something bold. You take a very public stand and show the world just how committed and in love you two are."

"A press conference?"

Jeff paused. Sometimes it amazed him how dense talent could be. "A covenant marriage."

"No..."

Jeff pressed on. "It says, 'this time it's for good. This time, it's for life.' People love that shit."

"No..."

"What do you care? It's marriage. It's not gonna feel any different. You're still gonna sleep in the same house. Still gonna eat the same food, go to the same parties –"

"You can't get divorced."

Jeff dismissed her with a wave of his hand. "Yes, you can get divorced. Why, you wanna get divorced again? How many times you gonna marry this guy?" She didn't smile. "I'm kidding. You can get divorced. It's just not as easy. But I mean, if he beats you or cheats on you..."

"Or I cheat on him?"

"Your words."

Myra dropped her napkin on her salad. "So what you're saying is, you want this as insurance that I don't mess up again."

Jeff smiled, looking around to see who was listening. "Calm down. Let's remember where we are."

"You brought it up."

"All I'm saying…Okay, I went about this all wrong…I'm sorry…all I meant was, if you guys *do* decide to do something bold – like a covenant marriage – it would go a long way to undo… "

"I've got a spin class." Myra stood up and signaled for the check.

"Okay, this wasn't the time…I'm sorry." Jeff reached for the check but Myra beat him to it. "Stop. What are you doing? The agency pays for this."

"No, I pay for this." She touched his tie. "And I pay for this." She picked up his cell phone. "And this. And everything else you like to put on display. So just remember who you're talking to when you make your snide little judgments about my private life."

"Come on, My," he said with a frozen grin,

"we don't want a scene…"

"It's exactly what you want." Myra dropped four fifties and exited.

What an ingrate, Jeff thought. *And after all I've done for her!*

◆ ◆ ◆ ◆ ◆

Four teachers. Tom Reiner was disappointed at the turnout. He knew it was a last-minute announcement, that people had only seen the signs for a day. And he supposed he'd lost a few faculty members who had prior commitments to other school clubs and teams. But four teachers? That's how many care about the moral character of their students?

Tom stepped to the front of the room. "Well, I won't keep you long." He didn't like speaking to groups, especially teachers, who were always a tough audience. "I have come to notice over these past many years that more and more of our kids are getting pregnant. More premarital sex – I guess that's a given. And more and more graduates are turning up at the reunions divorced. More broken marriages. I just counseled a little girl today…"

Tom caught the glare of the principal, Mrs. Angler, in the back of the room. She'd already spoken to him once this school year about his loose lips visa vi private counseling sessions. She felt his job was to be a sounding board for the student body, a sort of informal confessional as it were, and she didn't like her guidance counselor to breach the confidences of the students.

"Anyway, you all know the types of situations I'm talking about. And I thought, maybe we, as educators, have dropped the ball. Maybe there's something…"

The door opened and Miss Yoeste stepped in. Tom could feel his adrenaline rush. She signaled, "Please continue," and took a seat.

"Maybe there's a way to bring these kinds of issues into the curriculum. So I thought I would raise the question and see if there were any ideas…"

Nobody raised their hand.

Tom tried to engage them. "Maybe a course on marriage skills."

"Mr. Reiner." Mrs. Angler didn't bother to put up her hand. "I appreciate your intentions here. It's quite commendable. But as you know, the curriculum is set by the Board of Education."

"Of course. I didn't mean, a formal class. But possibly something extra-curricular. A seminar or a workshop…"

Mrs. Angler took a step forward, as she always did when she wanted to bring a conversation to a close. "Quite honestly, at first blush, it's hard to conceive of how we could make something like this work. The state has strict parameters."

"Well, I definitely understand what we're up against. But I honestly don't see this as religious subject matter. My feeling is – "

"Why don't you and I sit down about this tomorrow in my office, hm? I think that would be the more appropriate forum for a discussion like this. Say, 7:45?"

"Yes, ma'am."

Mrs. Angler grinned and exited. The other teachers slowly and silently gathered their things and filed out. Tom dripped humiliation. Was it his imagination, or were they purposely avoiding eye contact with him?

"It's a good idea." Tom was surprised to see Miss Yoeste still in her seat, offering a supportive smile. "Don't give up on it, Mr. Reiner. Fight the good fight."

"Thank you, Sandra."

"You'll keep me posted?"

"Absolutely."

Miss Yoeste stood, straightened her skirt and

walked out.

It was moments like this that made Tom absolutely hate himself.

Ken was in bed, asleep, when his iPhone texts began to chirp and chirp and chirp. He grabbed for the phone as he shook himself awake. *Twelve-thirty-two a.m.? What the fuck could this be about?*

It was about Myra and Derek. Apparently, they'd just been spotted at *The Comedy Store* seated in a corner VIP booth, laughing and necking. *Holy shit*, Ken exclaimed in his head. *They're back together?!*

The three separate text tips were from fairly good sources, he reasoned. But still...why would Myra and Derek be back together after everything that went down?

Ken tried to fall back to sleep, but that proved impossible. So he got out of bed and started working some sources. Did anyone hear anything about Myra and Derek?

Within minutes, the answers began coming in. Yes, Myra's friend Judy Leon had been talking to her about it. And Myra's publicist had been sworn to secrecy, but since Ken already seemed to know…

The PR guy spilled the beans.

Now, Ken went in for the kill. He dialed and waited…

"Feldman!"

"Ian. Hate to bother you so late…"

"No problema, mi amigo. Just wrapped a date with a Columbian beauty pageant queen. That country knows how to grow coffee beans and beauty queens. What can I do for ya?"

"Well, I hate to be the messenger. But have you heard anything about Myra getting back together with Derek?"

Ian laughed. "For a newsman, Ken, you're way behind the times. They've been shacking up together for weeks now."

"Really? How do you feel about that?"

"Hey, she was always on loan as far as I was concerned." Then Ian remembered his last conversation with Ken at Sky Bar. "Oh yeah, I thought we might go the distance for a while. But possession is 90% of the law, right? Now he's in possession of her. I wish them the best."

"So, where's that leave you and Derek?"

"Shopping for quotes again?"

Ken chuckled. "That's all I got in my life."

"How 'bout this: Two's Company. Three's a War Zone."

Six hours later, that headline hit the internet under *The Peephole* banner. And the world knew that Myra and Derek were a 'thing' again.

And that Ian and Derek were a thing no more.

Chapter 6

*T*om Reiner loved this moment of the day. Climbing into his car and driving out of the Downey High parking lot was more than just the end of a work day. It was the moment he ceased being "Mr. Reiner" and became comfortable again; became "Tom" again.

Tom usually didn't like to stop in town on his way back to the house. But today he shelved his dislike of the busy stores and the high schoolers in the streets. Forget whoever might recognize him and say "hi" – even though he truly despised those momentary lapses back into his guidance counselor persona – because today marks the next step. Today the new *Dinnertime University* catalogue comes out.

After Mrs. Angler put the kibosh on Tom's extra-curricular idea, he took little time moving to a new plan. If Tom can't teach family values and the sanctity of marriage at his little high school, he reasoned, he'll teach it in a more public arena –

continuing adult education. *Dinnertime University* is a privately owned franchise that markets short, eclectic, leisure interest courses to the general public. For $69 (plus a twenty dollar registration fee), the citizens of any city can take courses ranging from "Thai Cooking" to "How To Audition for TV Commercials" to "Writing Novels That Sell." Nothing is too extreme to be a *Dinnertime University* offering. "How to Seduce A Woman" is a perennial. "Meet and Marry the Millionaire of Your Dreams" always fills up. "Become a Private Eye in Your Spare Time" is mostly popular among the stalking crowd. Whereas "The Art of Kama Sutra Sex" draws single men and ugly couples.

Tom parked at the hydrant, grabbed one from the newspaper box and scanned the pages, flipping through sections: "Computer Skills"…"Recreation and Leisure"…"Entertainment Careers." Ahh, here it is: "Relationships." Tom scanned for his blurb. Not on the first page. Not on the second. Flipping through, he finally spotted it on page eleven.

Is a Covenant Marriage Right for You?

Engaged? Soon to be? Or married and thinking about renewing your vows? Whether you're headed down the aisle for the first time or for another try, it's time to consider the *lasting commitment* of a Covenant Marriage. Discover the ins and outs of covenants, and why one is right for *YOU*! Divorce is an epidemic, with over 65% of first time marriages ending within ten years. It takes more than love and good intentions to make a marriage last; it takes a serious, life-long commitment – the kind you'll feel when your beloved agrees to a covenant wedding. You'll learn how to ask for a covenant without making your partner feel trapped, and how to word your covenant so that it's legally airtight. From religious aspects to legal to emotional, we'll cover the essentials to start your new married life right...and keep it right! Come make the covenant choice, and start "forever" today!

Instructor: Tom Reiner, M.A.

Four Sessions, starts January 25, 6-8:30 p.m.

Tom Reiner has spent the last 22 years as a high school guidance counselor. He holds a Bachelor's degree in Theology from Boston University and a Masters in Education. Tom is a formerly happily married widower (hint, hint).

Tom got a sick feeling as he re-read the ad. Was it too righteous? Too editorialized? He was having second thoughts. *Did the joke at the end – "hint, hint" – even make sense? Or did it just come off as lonely and desperate?* Plus, he realized he'd forgotten to put the day of the week in, using the word "sessions" instead. *Damn! And why two and a half hours? Do I really need a full ten hours to sell people on the topic. The whole thing sounds too formal and dry, like a bad lecture series. Which maybe it's destined to be.*

Then he noticed the course blurb on the page opposite his...

Learn to Kill Your Spouse
(and Get Away With It!)

Can't stand him or her? Divorce not an option? Wishing "your better half" was a loving memory? Stop living with the pain and inconvenience of an unfaithful, insensitive or dull dull dull husband or wife and have the freedom you deserve. Acclaimed former murder suspect and acquitted defendant Helen Fay Crittenden will show you how to plan, prepare for and "execute" the perfect crime! This four week workshop will cover: where to find accomplices; dealing with police interrogators; 14 things your defense team didn't tell you; the do's and don'ts of DNA; six surefire places the cops will never search; alimony versus testimony; and the dirty truth about contract hits.

Instructor: Helen Fay Crittenden

Four Tuesdays, starts January 25, 7 pm-10 pm

Instructor Bio: *"Helen Fay Crittenden was accused, tried and acquitted of murdering her husband, and hence enjoys legal immunity from further prosecution for that crime, allowing her to speak openly and candidly on the subject. She has appeared on Court TV, Oprah, The Today Show, and numerous other media outlets in conjunction with that trial, and is currently writing a nonfiction account of her life (Bantam Books). Helen lives in Beverly Hills with her new husband and their Golden Retriever, Kitten."*

To Tom, this was exactly the mentality his course was designed to counteract. And now, he had to compete for students with a media sensation like Helen Fay Crittenden. Who's going to choose a course about commitment and fidelity when they can hear the most famous murderess of the century tell her cold-blooded story?

Reiner was thoroughly discouraged. *Ah, what the hell. Who's gonna sign up for a preachy class on marriage taught by a public school teacher? Not even a teacher, a guidance counselor. A public education bureaucrat.* Tom wished he'd had the guts to stick with theology – his first love – instead of opting for a "practical career," as his dad had advised him after graduation. But no, he never followed through. *The story of my life. All talk and pipe dreams, no action. Just like with Miss Yoeste. Never the backbone to...*

Tom's stomach knotted. He crumpled the catalog and tossed it in the trash.

◆ ◆ ◆ ◆ ◆

The idea of covenant marriages is not biblical, as Ken Feldman had previously believed.

With all its implicit moral sanctity, the concept of permanent marriages first seems to have surfaced as a twentieth century antidote to divorce. (Though the argument most certainly goes back as far as the societal ills it sought to address and man's ability to lay blame for those ills.)

The first modern political debate on record on the subject came in France, where a "Covenant Marriage Proposal" appeared as a 1947 amendment to the French Civil Code. A "Commission of Civil Code Reform" had been tasked to study revisions to the existing divorce codes. But a counter-proposal by a commission member named Henri Mazeaud sparked the most spirited debate. Mazeaud's proposal would have radically altered the institution of marriage in France by creating two distinct types of unions: dissoluble, and what he termed "insoluble."

Or, in the truest sense, 'Till death do us part.'

The key points Mazeaud used to justify his idea were to ensure that both parties had the same conception of a 'lifetime' commitment, avoiding single-parent families, deterring extra-marital affairs, and encouraging forgiveness and reconciliation when cheating did occur. To Ken, reading excerpts from the commission debate seemed as timely in the twenty-first century as they were eight decades before.

Fortunately for French couples, Mazeaud's amendment was voted down by the Commission, 12-9, and never became law.

Amazing, Ken thought. *But for two votes that might have gone the other way, a handful of tight-ass legislators in France might've upended the institution of marriage in their country and maybe for the rest of the western world. Hardly befitting the image of the French as happy warriors in the Monogamy Wars.*

But Ken knew that American legislators had also set their crosshairs on the topic of divorce. The movement seems to have started in 1990 when a Florida state representative named Daniel Webster introduced a covenant marriage bill in the state legislature. Webster's bill was even harsher than the ideas Mazeaud had promoted five decades prior, as it only allowed divorce in the case of adultery and further declared that if both spouses had ever cheated, divorce was back off the table and they would be stuck with each other for life. (Apparently Webster, the bloodline namesake of one of the most famous lawyers in American history, had no love lost for divorce lawyers.) The bill went nowhere, though it boosted his conservative bona fides enough to propel him to the state senate and eventually the U.S. House of Representatives.

Seven years later the idea had migrated to Louisiana in the body of Law Professor Katherine S. Spaht and Tony Perkins, then a rising state politician who would end up becoming the head of the infamously conservative Family Research Council. With lobbying help from the Catholic Church and the state's powerful Protestant community, they were able to push it through the legislature in 1997, bringing legally recognized and binding covenant marriages to the love birds of Louisiana and the shores of the United States. Arkansas and Arizona soon followed suit.

Though conservative politicians in other states seemed eager to ride the religious right wave to higher and higher offices by offering covenant bills of their own, there were few buyers in the marketplace of actual matrimony, as only the most extreme religious zealots would agree to a marriage that could bind you to a drunk, derelict or violent loser for life. But then the media did what it always does and glorified the worst of America for public consumption.

It happened on the night of April 1, when *The*

Tonight Show's silver-haired host Jimmy Fallon, still slogging along after all these years, officiated a covenant marriage on the air, featuring America's sweethearts Myra and Derek. The date was strategically chosen to make viewers wonder whether the whole thing was an elaborate April Fool's gag. But it wasn't.

It was the brainchild of super-agent Jeff Josephs, who had finally convinced Myra that her career depended on proving to the public that this marriage would last. In turn, she convinced the very dubious Derek that it was the only way he would ever see her vagina again.

Josephs came up with the idea of televising the wedding for maximum PR, and picked April 1st for the exact purpose of making the public bemused and curious, ensuring maximum tune-in. Fallon had been legally ordained to perform weddings using an online website, costing NBC all of $8.99. Then he lobbied his celebrity friends to hold the highly anticipated nuptials on his stage in the show's A-segment. Josephs had even pitched the idea of asking Ian to be the best man. But that stunt was a bridge too far for Derek, who warned, "Sure, as long as Jimmy's ready to officiate his funeral in the B-segment."

The affair (catered by TV celebrity chef Henri DeMott, a family friend of Myra's parents) drew the most viewers in late-night television history, and even made the list of top twenty-five rated TV shows of all-time. Admirers watched from every corner of the planet. They even received an unusual wedding gift from an Associate Justice of the Supreme Court: an antique Colt .45 revolver.

Soon, every bride-to-be wanted to be like Myra. If their intended was reluctant to agree to a covenant, they could simply argue, "Why can't you be more like Derek?"

No one will ever know how many of these new-fad Super Vow marriages were entered into under duress. But with social media promoting them, the religious right endorsing them, and Myra and Derek publicizing them with every red carpet appearance and *American Peephole* front page photo of their fairytale romance, the number of couples seeking covenant marriages exploded across the land. The fairytale should have been a cautionary tale. But in America, caution is often thrown to the wind.

Within a year came a deluge of covenant marriage bills offered in Missouri, Georgia, Alabama, Texas, Oklahoma, Ohio, Indiana, Utah,

Alaska, and anywhere else the extreme religious right could gain a foothold. Some passed, some did not; but like cockroaches, the bills just kept showing up again and again in similar forms.

The results were staggering. Prior to the Myra-Derek nuptials, there had been fewer than 8,000 covenant marriages nationally. A year later, the number was over 1.2 million and rising. The spate of covenant marriage requests in states that didn't officially recognize them grew as well, and with them a movement called 'The Covenant Crusades' was born.

Ken could remember when his own state, California, had been besieged by Covenant Crusaders. Like all bad ideas in California, it started as a grass roots movement in the form of petition for a ballot proposition, requiring several hundred thousand signatures to earn it a place on the ballot. Grass roots my ass, Ken thought back then, dodging score after score of clipboard toting, morality haranguing, sexually repressed Christian soldiers on every street corner and in every mall. The money behind this "grass roots" campaign was enough to wage political wars in ten states, let alone one. The media ad buys alone boosted California's economy by 3 per cent. But with a disciplined counteroffensive by the ACLU, buttressed by plenty of liberal Hollywood celebrity spokesmen for their cause, the saner people of the left coast were able to repel their legislature's efforts to enter their bedrooms by a razor-thin 50.1-49.5% vote.

The rightwing side dismissed the results as a throwback to California's liberal reactionary past.

The media reported it as a political thermometer but couldn't make heads or tails of its reading.

Only those on the winning side saw it for what it actual was: the clarion bell of impending doom.

Jerry Proud looked around the room. Six women, two men. Hmm. He wondered what that says, that three times as many women as men are interested in killing their spouse. Of course, Jerry wasn't there to learn how to kill Leslie, he told himself. He just liked murder mysteries, liked reading them, liked hearing about them. Like that Trey Scott case. And Helen Fay Crittenden.

When he had glanced through the *Dinnertime University* brochure, Jerry didn't know what he was looking for. A few classes seemed interesting at first glance. That private detective course could've been fun. Then he noticed a screenplay writing class. Jerry had always fancied himself a writer and thought he might enjoy taking a shot at Hollywood. He loved those shoot 'em up movies, especially the ones with surprise endings. A good Bruce Willis action story. Then he came across "Learn To Murder Your Spouse (And Get Away With It!)." Jerry had read the blurb five times, not believing the incredible bad taste. The nerve of this woman to profit off her husband's demise. He turned the page to look around – classes on poetry, covenant marriages, graphic design – but he was somehow drawn back to the Helen Fay Crittenden class description. Why not? She had the makings of a great movie, and her class might give him some inspiration for a murder story. Then, if he got juiced about it, he could take the screenwriting class next quarter.

Jerry looked at the women seated around him. *Not bad.* The plump black lady, she was definitely not his type. But the other five – *Not bad at all. Thirties and forties. Good figures. Probably married gals who're staying in shape for a current extramarital lover or in anticipation of future tryst.*

The tall, prematurely gray haired chick looked a little hardened and haute, with a huge diamond ring. *Just some rich bitch from the city,* he figured. The redhead, though – *she can't be more than 31, 33. Look at that face. Smooth skin, no makeup. Just the subtlest hint of crows' feet. And the legs!* Jerry loved exposed legs that didn't need stockings to look sheer. Jerry liked the way she held them, pressed together, not crossed, tucked at an angle under her chair. Very feminine. The green pleated skirt and black patent leather Mary Janes made her look like a schoolgirl. *Not bad at all!*

"Welcome!" Helen Fay Crittenden looked younger in person than she did on the witness stand. Jerry sort of had a thing for her during the televised trial. But now, she was positively doable. Five-six, about one hundred eighteen pounds, tiny waist. She seemed to have more on top these days, and most people would assume she'd had some work done since the trial. But Jerry read news coverage in *The American Peephole* and knew the truth: that Helen had taped her boobs down during the trial so as to be less sexually threatening to the female jurors. "I'm Helen Crittenden. Let's go around the room and meet each other, whaddaya say?"

Helen pointed to the rich lady. She hesitated, then spoke up.

"Fiona."

"No last name, Fiona? Or are you afraid being here will be used against you in court some day?" The class chuckled.

"Fiona Weintraub-Finch," she confessed through an unamused smile.

"Welcome, Fiona. Pleasure to meet you. And the woman behind her?" She pointed to the redhead in the green pleated skirt.

"Lisa Prococino."

Great voice, Jerry thought.

"Hi, Lisa What prompted you to take this course? Or should I say, *who* prompted you?" Titters.

"You. I read your book and was fascinated by your life. I guess I'm a fan."

"Well, thank you. And to her right? The man with no wedding ring?" She raised an eyebrow in mock suspicion, and the class laughed again. She has her shtick down like a standup, Jerry thought.

The man with no wedding ring smiled and

spoke. "Ken Feldman."

"Hi, Ken. And who are you planning to murder?"

"My editor, for telling me to take this course." More laughter.

"Editor?" For the first time, Helen seemed a bit unsettled.

"I write for *The American Peephole*?" Ken ended it as a question, as if he expected something. Helen was bemused. "We contacted – didn't your publicist call you?" Everyone could tell from her silence that the publicist had not told her. "We're doing an article on the class. I'm sorry. I hope this is okay with you. Your publicist approved it. Mike Sullivan? But if it makes you at all uncomfortable – "

Helen held her hand up and smiled. "No no, it's fine. I love reporters. Of course you're welcome in the class, Ken. I have nothing to hide." Then, with a wicked grin, "Any more." A huge laugh. She soaked it up – Helen Crittenden clearly likes the spotlight – and pointed to the man in the back row.

"Jerry Proud."

"Hi Jerry. And how did you come to our little

class?"

"My wife suggested it." The class roared. At first Jerry didn't know why that was funny. Then it hit him as the laughter continued. Even Helen Fay Crittenden couldn't help but chuckle.

"I want to know more about *your* marriage, Jerry," she purred. Another big laugh from the class.

Jerry smiled. He was already the center of attention. *This is gonna be fun after all!*

Chapter 7

$\mathcal{T}$om Reiner's Covenant Marriage course got all of two signups, and he was pissed when *Dinnertime University* cancelled it hours before the first class due to low enrollment. But they conceded that the course description might have hindered signups, so they agreed to offer the course again sometime in the future.

In the meantime, Jerry thoroughly enjoyed "Learn To Kill Your Spouse." Helen Crittenden was a hoot, he thought, with all those not-so-subtle hints about how she had offed her hubby and gotten away with it. And he had even gotten laid

It happened on the night of the third session. He had been placed in a two person group with Lisa Prococino, the redhead with the love of murder mysteries. They were paired for an assignment on how detectives try to pry a confession out of a murder suspect. Jerry was chosen to play the detective; Lisa the suspect. Each group was given a

list of the types of questions ("Prompts," Helen
called them) that might be asked, and tricks for
tripping up the person being interrogated ("the
Rules of Deniability," per Helen.) The suspect was
supposed to decide before the exercise if they were
indeed guilty or innocent, and were given certain
secret cues to use in each event.

Each team met privately to concoct the facts
of their "case." Then Helen asked for volunteers to
go first. Jerry and Lisa immediately threw up their
hands, and Helen invited them to the front of the
classroom. Lisa played her part to the hilt.

"Thank you for coming in today," Jerry
started out. "I know this is a difficult time for you.
This won't take long." That sounded like something
a detective would say, he thought. Lisa nodded,
acting the sad but not necessarily bereaved widow.
"So tell me, Ms. Prococino, about what time did
you arrive home the night of the murder?"
(Interrogator prompt 1: make the suspect commit to
facts and details.)

"Well, first of all, I wouldn't necessarily call
it murder," Lisa said, following Crittenden's Rule of
Deniability number 1: Never acknowledge the
crime. As soon as you do, it makes you look guilty.
"But I left around eight-fifteen and estimate I got

back around 10."

"And what did you find when you arrived home?"

"I came in through the garage door as I always do, dropped my packages on the kitchen counter, and called out 'I'm home' to my husband."

"Packages?"

"Yes. I had just gone grocery shopping. At the Whole Foods on Wilshire." Here Lisa was following suspect's Rule 2: Establish an airtight alibi. In this case, she was establishing that she had been in a store earlier that night, making it easier for her attorneys to argue reasonable doubt, should the case go to trial. But Jerry had paid attention in class, too.

"So, you have receipts for these groceries?"

"Yes."

Jerry smiled. "Good. We'll need those for the time stamp. And we'll need your credit card number to check the purchase against." Jerry knew that with that statement, Lisa had just opened herself up to a police review of ALL her recent credit card purchases, which might reveal some other incriminating evidence. Interrogator prompt 2: Establish new lines of evidence that could contest the suspect's story.

"I'll have to ask my attorney about that," Lisa coyly countered.

"You can, but it won't make a difference. You just gave us probable cause to subpoena them." Jerry stood up and walked around Lisa's chair, hoping to make her nervous. He loved this game. "Now, tell me what transpired next?" Jerry thought using the word "transpired" made him sound more like a detective.

"Well, it's all such a blur." (Suspect's Rule 4: Establish a faded or faulty memory of innocent facts, so if they catch you in a lie, you can claim that was a mistake of memory, too.) "I walked through the living room, called Dennis's name, and proceeded into the bedroom, where I found him."

"And how did you 'find' Dennis?" Jerry said it in a way as to suggest he was skeptical.

"Well, at first I saw a ladder by the bed, under the ceiling fan. Which of course was unusual. Then I saw him on the floor by the bed. Bathed in blood. And his head had this big…"

"Gaping hole?"

"Wound. As if he'd hit it on something."

"He'd hit his head? Not 'as if he'd been hit by something?'"

Lisa didn't respond. Rule 3: When you don't

have something to say, say nothing."

"And what else did you find?"

"A hammer. Lying nearby." Lisa dropped a hammer into the facts of her fictional murder case in homage to Helen, who had famously found her husband drowned at the bottom of their Bel Air pool with traces of Ativan in his system and an unexplained two-prong claw hammer wound on his right temple.

"Laying nearby. 'Lying' is what people do when they are afraid of the truth." Jerry loved that ad-lib; it accomplished Interrogator Prompt 3: put the suspect on the defensive. Plus, he thought it sounded like something a TV cop might say to shake up a suspect. Though actually it was his English that was shaky; 'lying nearby' is technically correct.

"Two more minutes," Helen Crittenden beckoned from the audience, urging her student cop to wrap up his interrogation.

"Any other questions for me, Lieutenant?"

Jerry leaned in. "So your story, the one you want us to believe, is that while you were out 'shopping for groceries' at nine at night, your husband just 'decided' to fix the squeaky ceiling fan? And somehow fell off the ladder and onto his hammer, smashing his own skull in three places?"

"Or on the footboard of the bed. Or the wood platform. Or all three. Hence three wounds."

"And how exactly would he hit all three in one fall?" Interrogator Prompt 4: make the suspect explain themselves. Details are a suspect's worst enemy.

"It's a reasonable inference," Lisa purred back. "All I know is what I found when I came home. I'm sure once you and the medical examiner study the evidence, you'll come to the same conclusion."

Lisa was good! Dropping the word 'reasonable' in her statement meant it would be in the official record for the jury to hear and repeat when they were reviewing the evidence. (Rule 6.) And though her story about her husband falling on his hammer and bashing in his own head three times seemed far-fetched, she knew that all her defense team had to do was find one retired medical examiner to agree that it was possible. Not probable, but just conceivable. That would create enough reasonable doubt that she had killed her husband earlier that evening. (Rule 5.)

"And how do you explain your fingerprints on the murder weapon and the ladder?" Prompt 5:

Once the suspect is committed to the details of their story, contest it with the facts.

"Again, detective, I disagree with this assumption that it was a murder. It's my house. I happen to be very handy. I often used the hammer to hang pictures, and the ladder to dust the ceilings, change lightbulbs. I just wish my darling Dennis had left fixing the fan for me that night. He'd still be with me today." On that, Lisa broke down in tears. Their classmates applauded.

"Wonderful!" Helen exclaimed. "I couldn't have done it better myself." Everyone laughed.

"Lisa, Jerry, take your seats. Let's go over how each one scored points."

Lisa stood up and hugged Jerry, who tingled at the warm rush of her embrace. It was the hottest thing to happen to him in years. As they walked back to their seats, her hand grazed his. It was subtle, but Ken Feldman noticed; it was more than an accidental touch.

After class, other students kept complimenting Jerry and Lisa on their interrogation improv, and Jerry basked in the glory.

Walking out, Lisa caught up with him.

"You missed your calling. You should've been a cop."

"And you missed yours."

"You mean, I should've been a murderer?"

"An actress. You were amazing up there. Ever do any acting?

"Just in high school. I toyed with the idea of maybe going into modeling. But I ended up going into clinical psychology instead."

"Well, you've got the talent to be an actress. And the looks." Jerry thought that was a smooth line.

Lisa winced inside at his ham-fisted flirting. But there was something about him that was sort of adorable. So she took the bait.

"I notice you're wearing a ring. I hope you didn't take this class with something un-kosher in mind."

"Nothing in my mind is kosher," he smiled. "I'm gentile through and through."

"So tell me, Lieutenant, do you ever have drinks with a murder suspect?"

"Only the guilty ones."

Lisa laughed, then took his hand and led him to her apartment ten blocks away, making small talk as they went.

"So what made you choose this course," Jerry inquired, not recalling Lisa's intro from the first night of class.

"I'm fascinated by true crime stories and murderers. Something about the psychology of it. The purity of trying to commit the perfect crime. What about you?

"Oh, the same, I guess," Jerry parried back. He couldn't tell her that in truth he sometimes fantasized about offing his own wife.

"I know! Isn't it fascinating?! Have you ever thought about how you would kill someone and get away with it?"

"No," Jerry lied. "Not really."

"I have."

"And how would you do it?

"By car. Something like 35,000 people die in car accidents in the U.S. every year. And some 17% of those are pedestrian deaths. So, you already have a presumption of accidental death built in."

"Yeah, but if you run over someone you know…"

"Alibi? Easy-peasy. You just say you hit the gas peddle instead of the brake. Cops call them "wrong peddle" accidents. They happen a lot more than you think. Fifteen times a month, according to the NHTS, mostly in parking lots. And 60% of them are caused by female drivers, so I have a built-in advantage." She laughed.

"Wow, you're really done your homework."

"I told you – it's my passion."

"I'd probably try to make it look like someone else did it, like a burglar or a jealous lover. That way you get to really beat the snot out of them after she's dead and you can blame it on someone else."

"She?"

"I mean, they…them…after they're dead."

"Ah. But then you have all that messy forensic evidence to worry about.

"That's what raincoats and gloves are made for."

They both shared a good-natured laugh as they turned up the steps of Lisa's building, where they continued to role-play the suspect and the cop in a conversation laced with sexual double-entendres.

"So? Is this the scene of the crime?" Jerry asked, glancing in her bedroom.

"Why officer! I hope you have a search warrant."

"I only search when there's 'probable cause'," he came back, sliding his finger down the front of her neck. And down further.

Four shots of tequila later (one for him, three for her), she was kicking off her shoes and unzipping his pants.

Jerry, for his part, clumsily tried to undo her bra and fumbled with her skirt zipper. To his delight there were no panties to negotiate; Lisa was going commando that night.

"I'm sorry, Lieutenant, it looks like I forgot to wear my department issued panties. I hope you won't demote me."

Jerry hadn't been with another woman since he'd been married. Oh, he fantasized about it all the time. But here was a very real, very beautiful woman letting him undress her and role-playing with him. *Leslie would never do this*, he thought between kisses. When you're married, sex becomes more of a routine. Even the hottest couples can fall into bad sexual habits in marriage. The worst, Jerry felt, was the evening bathroom routine. When you're single you enter the bedroom already kissing and lunge into bed. After marriage, you have to go through all that pre-bedtime rigamarole women insist on doing. Removing makeup and combing out hair and lotions and pills. Then comes the toothbrushing. Watching her power-wash her mouth with all that foamy gunk. It looked like a carwash!

By the time Leslie was in bed for the night, Jerry could barely get it up. Now here was a woman backing him into her bedroom again, and he was rock hard and ready to party.

After a few minutes of rushed foreplay – mostly so she could lubricate his 'baton' – she mounted him on her red velvet divan and rode him till he climaxed. The entire event took less than five minutes.

To Jerry, it felt like heaven. To Lisa, it immediately felt like a mistake.

He was wrong. She was right.

Derek and Myra were still on their honeymoon in Saint Lucia when he sensed this whole re-marriage thing had been a terrible idea. The press, who'd found out where they were honeymooning, were hounding them constantly. Myra seemed distant and less-than-affectionate. And when they did make love, he couldn't get the mental image of her and Ian fucking out of his mind.

Ken Feldman had tried to get The Peephole to finance a trip for himself to Saint Lucia to cover the world's most famous couple. But his cheapskate managing editor preferred to use local stringers to get the photos. Meaning Ken had to write his pieces based on rumors and second-hand gossip.

What he was hearing from his sources – employees at the resort, friends of the newlyweds, and from Ian himself, who maintained mutual friends with them – was that Myra had been very hurt when Ian dumped her, and she had run back to Derek on the rebound. Derek had missed his main squeeze, but also felt the need to prove to himself that he could win her back from his former best friend-cum-romantic rival. Once he had bed Myra a few times and realized that something fundamental had changed for them between the sheets, he had soured on their relationship and on the covenant marriage bullshit that their agents had backed them into. Now he was hoping she'd cheat on him so he could get out of this hellish situation.

Myra had always loved Derek, and only strayed from him because Ian had seduced her. But once she had dined off the menu of Ian's famous sex techniques, she was hooked. Ian was insatiable in the bedroom, and he stayed hard well past when other men like Derek would call it a night. Or morning. Or afternoon delight.

The other thing Ian brought to his lovemaking was his studded tongue. He had it pierced when he was nineteen, and because he had learned to speak with the tiny ball stud without any noticeable diction faux pas, few people knew he had one. But in the bedroom, it became his saber, a weapon he used deftly to defrost even the most frigid of females. His ability to find the right spot — be it on a nipple, navel or clitoris – and tease it to the point of climax, was extraordinary. Once he had brought a woman to orgasm once or twice with his tongue, actual intercourse became the icing on their cake. Most women struggled to achieve climax before her man finished. But with Ian, you were already satisfied – often multiple times – before he even entered you. That took the pressure off for Myra, who usually did have some trouble getting to the final curtain. But Ian took her there effortlessly, giving her a long, deep tissue massage from deep inside – one that she felt in every muscle in her body. Their extended coitus left her physically spent and emotionally fulfilled beyond her wildest dreams.

Yes, she still felt love for Derek. But she resented that he had left her for a movie shoot, and left her in the hands of his bestie. He had even asked Ian to wine and dine her while he was gone. What did Derek think would happen?!

What woman would ask her drop-dead gorgeous best friend to spend intimate time with her man while she was out of town? Only a man could think he was so sexy and desirable that his lady would never think to find pleasure elsewhere. And only a male movie star would hand off his prize possession to a man like Ian Braydon for caretaking. It was like handing him the keys to his Lamborghini Roadster to turn it over and warm up the engine, and expecting him not to take her out for a spin.

Ian had taken Myra out for a spin. And another. And another. Now she wanted to be driven by him and only him. He knew how to throttle her up and pace her to the finish line.

Whereas Derek only knew how to back her out of the driveway and maybe get her to third gear.

A few months into the young marriage, Myra was texting with Ian again. She wanted him, but knew that if she screwed up this marriage, she'd be screwing up her career forever.

So they devised a plan to get Derek to cheat first. Then she could publicly blame their eventual breakup on him. All they had to do was find the right bait.

Better yet, jail bait. Catch him in the act with some underage girl. That would definitely make

Derek the heavy and Myra the innocent victim.

Yes, a covenant marriage made fixing matrimonial mistakes infinitely more difficult. But where there's a will…

◆ ◆ ◆ ◆ ◆

"OMG! You'll never guess what just happened!" Such was the start of a text thread between Lorraine Ann Leaver and her friend, Charlotte.

"Do tell," Charlotte typed back.

"I just got a dick pic from Derek Chase! "

Lorraine loved emojis and peppered them into almost every text.

"Yeah, right," came Charlotte's reply.

"Dead serious. Wanna see?"

"What, you're gonna send me some guy's junk and tell me it's Derek Chase?

"It is! He gave me his digits and everything!!"

"You're drunk."

"Maybe. But I got the pic and the message on my phone Maybe I better not forward it, just in case it's a virus or something 😣 Come over and I'll show you!!! 🚴 🚗 ✈️

What Lorraine was bragging about was indeed a dick pic of Derek Chase, surreptitiously taken by Myra while her husband was sleeping off a bender. The text was from Myra too, sent from Derek's phone, using the facial recognition feature to open it up during said bender blackout.

"Hi there," the text message began. "My name is Derek Chase. Yes, that one. Really. I was scanning Instagram and came across your profile and photos. Really cute!! And you don't live that far from me. Any chance we could hook up sometime?" Then followed two glam shots of Derek's flaccid but still impressive member – one close up and one angled to include his face. His eyes were shut, but Myra had ever-so-gently placed his hand near his rod so it would appear he was in the throes of self-passion, hence the closed eyes. Together they proved that movie star Derek Chase had indeed sent a series of texts to this sixteen year-old stranger. And Lorraine was just young enough and naive enough to believe it was legit.

Eighteen minutes later, Charlotte was in Lorraine's bedroom, starring at the photos and text in disbelief.

"Are you gonna answer him?"

"What do you think? Of course I am. What should I say?"

"This can't be real," Charlotte said as she handed back the phone. "Why would he text you?"

"Uh, hello!"

"I mean, okay, you're cute and everything. But Derek Chase? He's got Myra. And probably every other gorgeous actress in Hollywood. So, I query again: why YOU?"

"What difference does it make? He did. That's all that counts."

Charlotte was approaching this far more analytically than her star-struck friend. That's what Myra was hoping for.

Myra had spent three days scouring Facebook for just the right stooge. First, she had to be drop-dead stunning. Lorraine fit that bill. Next, she had to be Derek's type: blonde, busty, and with glutes that show no mercy. Check! The plethora of photos of Lorraine in bikinis were a testament to that. Then, she had to be geographically desirable. That meant close enough that Derek would be able to find and fuck her, but far enough away from Hollywood that he'd think he could get away with it. Living about an hour's drive away from Derek's home in Pacific Palisades, Lorraine also checked that box.

Next, she had to be dumb enough to fall for it. The combination of mindless "joke" memes and semi-coherent posts peppered with emojis that Lorraine had spent the past year of her life composing seemed to lay claim to her being one of the most naive, ill-informed teenagers this side of *PEN15*.

Finally, and most important criteria of all, she had to be a minor but look several years more mature. This was the toughest part. Myra had spied a lot of 17 year-olds who fit the bill. But she and Ian had determined that 17 wasn't young enough to villainize Derek in the eyes of the public. No, he needed to be caught screwing around with a real minor – 16 or younger – to make sure that when Myra filed for divorce from their covenant marriage, no one would take his side.

In Lorraine Leaver, she found the ultimate jailbait. A girl sixteen and three months who could easily pass for 20 or 21, who had the body of a runway model, the face of an angel, and the survival instincts of a stray puppy. Myra knew Lorraine was his type because before she hooked up with him,

Myra had seen the other girls he'd dated. Mostly clones of Lorraine. No, the bait was perfect. All Derek needed was opportunity and motive. And Lorraine was the picture-perfect opportunity.

Now she needed the motive.

"Since I showed myself to you, maybe you can return the favor. I saw lots of great s of you on your page, but all that clothing! I'd 🤍 to know what the real you looks like…without all this 👗 👕 👖 👙 😉"

Myra made sure to use a lot of emojis so as to speak in Lorraine's native tongue.

As she expected, within minutes came a response. Three honey shots of Lorraine sprawled on her bed, au natural. Followed by a line of emojis that made no sense whatsoever, signed "xoxo, Lorraine."

The motive!, Myra sighed. No way he doesn't light up to that.

Now came the final act of phase one. Myra quickly deleted the opening text from the thread on Derek's phone, so he didn't see the incriminating opening lines that he had never composed. All he would see in the morning was a handful of stunning nude shots from some hot girl named Lorraine attached to that phone number.

Myra put the iPhone back down on Derek's nightstand and got back into bed on the other side.

Her plot to rid herself of this albatross of a husband was in motion. It might take a week or two for things to progress to a point where a private detective could catch her husband and his juvenile mistress in a few compromising positions. But once she had the photographic evidence in hand, she could funnel it to a snake like Ken Feldman at The American Peephole and ensure that her path out of this covenant prison and back to Ian's bed would be legal and popular with her fans.

Chapter 8

*I*f bad luck were a commodity, Tom Reiner thought, *I'd be a billionaire.* Only nine days after his class was cancelled, two of the biggest movie stars in the world entered into a covenant marriage on national TV. Not having been much of a pop culture consumer himself, he barely knew the names Myra Dreyer and Derek Chase. But it was all his students were talking about, in the hallways, the lunchroom, and even during detention, which Mr. Reiner proctored on Mondays, Wednesdays and Fridays. That's what a teacher with no social life does with his time.

So, after school one day he drove down to the minimart behind the Gulf station to grab a *Peephole* and see what the fuss was about. Sure enough, he learned that America's sweetest sweethearts had re-married after a messy affair and had opted for a Super Vow wedding to ensure they'd never split again. *This!* Tom thought. *This is what I have to tap into for my class. If I could get one or both of them to make an appearance – or even just endorse it with a short blurb – I'd have 25 enrollees, and a wait list twice as long.*

But with only two months before the next *Dinnertime University* course catalogue went online, Tom knew he'd have to act fast. Tom really didn't know much about Hollywood people or how to contact them. But he remembered that Miss Yoeste had once talked about having a brother who worked in a movie studio publicity department. Maybe she might have some ideas. Plus, he relished any chance he got to talk to her.

So, in the teacher's lounge the next day, Tom casually asked Sandra Yoeste if her brother might know either of these two Hollywood superstars.

"Bobby? I don't know. I mean, I don't think he works directly with the actors in the movies he promotes. But it's possible. Why?"

Tom looked around the room. The other teachers were now eavesdropping on the conversation, and he didn't want it to get back to Mrs. Angler that he was talking up his *Dinnertime University* course on school grounds.

"Well, uh, it's a private matter."

He looked around the room at the other teachers listening in. Miss Yoeste followed his eyes and got the message.

"Oh. Well...would you like to meet for coffee after school to discuss it?"

Holy Jesus! Did she just ask me out?! "Sure!" Tom had to dial back his enthusiasm so he didn't sound like a girl who'd just been asked to the prom. "Uh, did you have someplace in mind?"

"It doesn't matter. Let's meet at your car after last period and find some place together."

She did! And she wants me to drive!!

"Oh... sure...fine. My car, 3:30."

"It's a date," Miss Yoeste smiled back as she bit into a chocolate donut and exited.

It's a date. Tom knew she had said that in jest. But to him, it was an actual, flesh-and-blood date.

Precisely at 3:30 pm, Tom arrived at his car. But he was alone. *Ah shit! She had second thoughts.*

You always do this! You come on too strong and by the time-

Before he could finish his thought, Tom saw Sandy Yoeste walking toward his Honda Accord. She was lovely as always, in a tailored brown pantsuit that made her look more like a Board of Ed supervisor than a plain ol' geometry teacher.

"Hi," he called as she approached. "I really appreciate you taking the time."

"Nonsense. This is long overdue," she said back. Her smile was so soft and sweet. Does she even know how adorable she is? That's when Tom began to panic. *Maybe she isn't doing this to help me out or because she likes me. Maybe she thinks that I have something to do with tenure decisions. And she's playing me to lock in her job.* But Tom quickly realized that was too paranoid for even him. Surely a smart cookie like Sandy Yoeste knows that a lowly guidance counselor has no pull whatsoever with the Board of Education that makes those decisions. After all, she's a math teacher. She knows that anything multiplied by a zero like me comes out to zero.

In the car, they chatted about their day and a few students that they had mutually worked with to try and get them back on track academically. About four blocks away on Lakewood Boulevard, Yoeste spotted a Golden Corral restaurant and pointed at it.

"Is Golden Corral okay? I could eat something if you aren't in too much of a rush."

"Uh…yeah, sure. I have some time." Then, trying to impress her, "Or, you know, we could go someplace nicer if you like. This is on me, so…"

"Oh no, I couldn't let you do that."

"Please," he shot back. "You're helping me out."

"Well…okay!"

She smiled at him a million-dollar smile as he passed the Golden Coral and headed to someplace swanky. "You like Macaroni Grill?"

"Sure," she exclaimed. "I love Italian!"

Once seated in Macaroni Grill (Tom asked for a window booth to up the ante), Miss Yoeste quickly perused the menu, then asked asked what looked good to him.

"Don't say what you're thinking, moron," he coached himself. "Um, I'm thinking about the chicken piccata. You?"

"You read my mind."

"Care to share an appetizer?"

"Oh, you are a mind reader, Mr. Reiner. Do you like bruschetta?"

"Yes. And please call me Tom."

"Thanks, Tom. This is fun!" The waiter came by with some water and bread, and she ripped into a garlic roll. "So, what did you want to know about my brother for?" She immediately put her hand over her mouth, as if she had burned it on something. *Could the bread be that hot?* he wondered.

"Did that sentence really come out of my mouth? God, you must think I'm a moron or something."

"Hey, listen, neither of us are English teachers. Relax. This is strictly off-duty."

"You're sweet. So, why did you ask about Bobby?"

"Well, you probably remember that I had toyed with the idea of hosting a club or seminar after school about covenant marriages."

"Yes, I was at the meeting."

"Well, after talking it over with Freida..." Tom used Mrs. Angler's first name to impress the young teacher. "...we mutually agreed that the logistics of doing it at school were too difficult. Insurance and whatnot."

"Insurance?" Sandra repeated while buttering the rest of her roll.

God, what a stupid stupid thing to say! Why

would there be insurance issues with a school club about marriages? Think, Tom, think!

Luckily, the waiter came back to take their order, shifting the focus away from Tom's verbal fart. Once they were done ordering...

"Anyway, I decided that a better venue for the topic would be a class at *Dinnertime University.* So I contacted them and got approved—"

"What a great idea!"

"Thank you. But it all came together so late that we couldn't really promote the course properly for next quarter. So we pushed it back to the following semester, which starts in a few months."

"A few months. Okay." Yoeste had no idea where this was going.

"And then I heard about this big wedding on The Tonight Show with that celebrity couple. And I thought, man!, if I could get one or both of them to speak at the course..."

"About their marriage..."

"Yes, exactly. I figure, with their names attached to the course, attendance would go through the roof. Then I remembered you had once said something about your brother working in the movie business."

"Ohh. You want Bobby to ask them about it."

"Exactly."

"Gee, I don't know." The waiter arrived with her Diet Coke, and she took a sip. "I mean, maybe he could. I really don't know a lot about what he does. But why would two movie stars drive to Downey just to talk to some *Dinnertime University* class? Nothing personal, mind you."

"Well, they clearly are passionate about the subject. Otherwise they wouldn't have chosen a covenant marriage and wouldn't have held it on national TV."

"True," she said, followed by another sip.

"Bruschetta?" the waiter inquired, holding the plate.

"Yes, thanks." Tom answered confidently to show he was an alpha male.

"Yeah, I watched it myself. Jimmy Fallon was so funny, wasn't he?" She tore into a slice of the toasted bruschetta.

"I didn't see it."

"Oh, you gotta find it online. His facial expressions during their vows were priceless."

"Be that as it may, if we could get Myra or David…"

"Derek."

"What did I say?"

"You said David."

"Oh. My bad. If we could get Myra or Derek to just call into the class on Zoom. Or even just write a blurb I could add to the course description."

"Well, now you're sounding more realistic. Though I hear things aren't so rosy in their marriage after all." She picked tomatoes off his untouched piece of bruschetta.

"Take it. It's yours."

"Oh no, you should try some. It's delicious."

"But if you'd like it…"

"Mr. Reiner, you're too sweet. You know, I never believed the things students said about you."

"The students say bad things about me?"

"Oh. No. Not 'bad.' More like…" She was stuck. "I just don't think they really understand your job, is all I meant."

"No. Nobody really understands what a guidance counselor does all day. Half the time I'm a psychologist, and half the time I'm the guy in the hallway who breaks up fights and tells them not to throw lit cigarette butts in the trash cans." She laughed at that, assuming he was trying to be funny. He wasn't. "Which doesn't leave much time for what I'm really here for…"

"Which is?"

"Well, which is to provide career and life guidance. To make sure they achieve their academic requirements, year by year. So we can get them out of our little secondary education hell-hole and into college or some kind of job when they graduate."

"The chicken piccata for the lady. Annnd for the gentleman, chicken piccata." The waiter put Tom's plate down with a smile, as if he had made the funniest quip in the world.

"Thank you."

"Parmesan Cheese?"

"No thanks," she waved him off. Tom did the same. "Dig in."

"Bon appetit," she said softly.

"Bon appetit." They both dug in.

"Mmm, yummy!"

Tom nodded, caught in a bite of capellini that was hanging down to his plate.

"So anyway," Tom returned after slurping the loose strands of pasta into his mouth, "...do you think your brother could be of any help?"

"I'll definitely ask. I'll call him tonight," she said before taking in another forkful of chicken ensconced in capellini.

Man, this woman can really eat!

"I'd appreciate that." They paused the

conversation to do a little more damage to their entrees.

"I gotta tell you, Sandy, this is very nice."

"Thank you Mr.— Thank you, Tom. It is nice. I don't really get to socialize with the other teachers much. I mean, not that we are fraternizing or anything. I know this is strictly a business meal."

"Well, it can be both a business meal and a pleasant meal. We can be teachers at work and still be friends off campus."

"I'd like that." She smiled a smile that made him want to order her dessert.

"Me, too," he smiled back.

"Can I ask you something, Tom?"

"Sure. Anything."

"Is Mr. Brody single?

"Dominick Brody in the English Department?"

"Yes. Do you know if he's involved or anything?"

"Uh, no…I don't think so. Why?"

"No reason. I was just wondering."

Oh fuck! She's into Brody and wants the scoop on his availability! Shit. That's why she was so eager to corner me out of school. Fuck Fuck Fuck!

"You like Mr. Brody?" Tom said it in his most feigned casual tone.

"What? No. He seems nice, though. But no. I know the rules about dating fellow teachers."

"Yes. So do I," he retorted in his most authoritarian voice. *If it was Dominick Brody she wanted to fuck, fuck her! Now that she knows I know, she won't dare go near him.*

"Wow, this is so nice, Tom." She raised her Diet Coke glass in mock cheers.

"Yes. Yes it is." *Fuck her!*

Jerry Proud tried calling and texting Lisa every day for the next three weeks. But she was ghosting him. Even in their final *Dinnertime* class together, she waited to see where he sat and grabbed a chair as far away from him as possible, then ignored him during breaks and after class.

Meanwhile, things at home had taken a turn for the worse. Leslie didn't find it amusing that Jerry was taking a class about killing your spouse. And she surely didn't find it funny when he returned home after class three at 1:30 in the morning. They were barely speaking now, and the kids also seemed distant and morose to their stay-at-home dad.

Moreover, Leslie had opened up a new bank account that was solely in her name, and was having her paycheck direct deposited into it. Before that, she would deposit her waitressing money into their joint account, and Tom could dip into it whenever he needed to, like for rent or Happy Meals for the kids or new fishing equipment, a gift to himself that he treated himself to quite often. Now he needed to go to Leslie for household cash, and she was like Scrooge with her separate earnings.

Was there a reason she was squirreling away money? Did she know about him cheating with Lisa? Or his secret wishes to cheat with Ms. McKenzie-Jenrette-Wallace? Or any of the other half dozen women he would secretly masturbate to? She had once walked in on him in the shower while he was doing Myra Dreyer in his mind. But he quickly covered his erection with a hand towel and claimed he was just wiping off some conditioner that had dripped off his head. Did she know about his masturbatory sex life and plan to break their covenant vows over that?

Or maybe – *maybe* – she opened the separate account because she wasn't earning a lot. Maybe she had stopped taking diner shifts so she could secretly meet some bucking bronco of a stud herself and ride his pony for hours on end.

Was Leslie cheating on him? Would that be the ultimate insult? What if she was fucking around behind his back while banking all her earnings to spring a surprise divorce on him, planning on using his own infidelity as the extenuating circumstances? Then she could sue him for alimony and child support. On his meager salary!!

Maybe it was time to consider what he had learned in the Helen Fay Crittenden course and think through all his options.

Ken Feldman was hearing a lot of rumors about Derek and Myra, and Myra and Ian, and Ian and Derek. Most of the rumors spoke of one cheating on the other or threatening to kill the other. Yes, there were even rumors and Derek and Ian were secretly shacking up. There was one delicious rumor that had the three of them had renting a house in Malibu where they were secretly living a very happy polyamorous life.

Ken didn't buy any of it. Derek and Ian go too far back together to suddenly be trading death threats or rubbing dicks together. And there'd be no reason for Ian to threaten Myra or her to threaten him, as they both didn't seem to want anything to do with each other at the end of their torrid affair. And Derek threatening Myra or Myra threatening Derek was a complete non-started; he figured her to be a rather delicate and fragile flower in private. No, Ken knew the people he reported on, and as quirky as these three were, none of them were into violence, that much he was sure of.

However, one rumor did catch his attention. He heard that Derek and Myra's covenant marriage agreement had been secretly drafted by the studio lawyers to be more ironclad than any covenant marriage previously on record, one that could only be dissolved if one party could produce physical evidence of an extra-marital affair or a threat of physical violence. That was rare for covenants, as the majority also allowed dissolution for physical and emotional abuse, or moral depravity of some kind, or abandonment.

But here was the kicker. According to the rumor, the legal wording in the document, put together by their respective Hollywood talent agencies with the help of their entertainment attorneys, was so severe that the "out clause" established that the parties – including the two talent agencies – could be sued for compensatory damages if that party were to cause the marriage to falter due to cheating or physical violence. And those damages could add up to eighty percent of the other party's lifetime income and earnings. What does that mean in layman's terms? It meant if one of them got caught cheating or beating the other, they would be on the hook for eighty percent of their projected yearly earnings FOR LIFE. Which could add up to hundreds of millions of dollars. Even if their careers subsequently went in the toilet, the damages would be based on an equation that uses their current earnings and projects them out fifty years. That's a world of hurt!

If true, Ken knew, it was an insane deal for anyone to have agreed to, let alone two highly erratic soulmates like Derek and Myra. But the gossip mill said the agencies had put tremendous pressure on the couple to agree to those terms, and when the two biggest talent agencies in the world (Galaxy Talent Agency and Marquee7 International) team up against two twenty-something actors with no real business savvy, they don't have much leverage to fight back.

Ken had first heard the rumor from a couple of girlfriends of Myra's, but he put little stock in their word as he knew these girls would say anything for a line of cocaine. Then Ken heard it again, but this time from a paralegal at one of the two entertainment law firms that had drafted the document. She told Ken she had reviewed the document herself and thought about surreptitiously nabbing photos of the most onerous clauses. But then she thought better of the idea, telling Ken, "People in this town have been killed for less."

Now Ken was truly intrigued. And damn it, he wanted to see that document. But how? Ken figured there were probably only a handful of copies of it in existence. Derek would have one. Myra would too, if she was smart. Their agencies each would have one. And their attorneys would too. That made six copies and Ken only needed one. Of course, those hard copies would be kept in locked file cabinets or safes, and the only people with access to them were ones who couldn't be bought off with the crummy tipster fees that a media rag like The Peephole could afford.

But Ken knew something else. People in Hollywood could be incredibly stupid and careless – even the very smart ones. You don't get taken down like Harvey Weinstein was without being careless. And Harvey was considered brilliant.

Yup, Ken figured, if a document like that was being passed from agency to agency, lawyer to lawyer to mark up, it was probably being passed around electronically. Which meant emails. Which meant an electronic trail.

If Ken could find some way to hack into the servers of one or more of the players, he had a better than fifty-fifty shot of finding a digital copy of the Chase-Dreyer covenant.

Now Ken put on his most devious reporter's thinking cap. Who could he get to hack into the files of the biggest talent agencies and law firms in L.A.? It had to be someone with the technical prowess, of course. But it also had to be someone with few moral scruples. And someone he could afford.

That's when Ken had an epiphany. There was a guy in the Helen Fay Crittenden course he had taken who, Ken seemed to recall, said he worked in cybersecurity. Some kind of salesman or something like that. The guy – Shit, what was his name? – had demonstrated through his classroom comments that he had the moral foundation of an ant and the personal scruples of that ant's ass. Plus, he didn't dress or present himself as particularly financially well-off or even doing okay. What was his name?! If Ken could just get that guy—

"Jerry!"

"What?," the sports and gaming reporter in the cubicle next to Ken's asked.

"Nothing. I was just trying to remember someone's name. Jerry. Jerry Proud."

"What is he, some kind of tipster or lead?"

"He just might be. Yeah."

"Mr. Reiner?"

Tom heard the knock on his door, but didn't look up. "My office hours don't start until two."

"But I have Miss Yoeste at two," implored Lorraine Leaver. "And I could really use your guidance about something very important."

Tom sighed and took off his glasses. No one respects office hours anymore. He dropped the specs on his desk and looked up. "What is it, Lorraine?"

"May I come in? It's a private conversation."

"Fine."

"Is it okay if I close the door? It's kind of a sensitive subject."

"Sure. Whatever." Tom indicated to the chair in front of his desk.

Lorraine closed the door behind her and sat

down. "Well, I know you're big into this covenant marriage thing and all. I saw your flyer."

"My flyer. Yes. Why, you thinking of getting married at sixteen?" Tom really didn't like to be bothered by students without appointments.

"No, of course not. I just wanted to know…

"Yes?"

"This is kind of difficult."

"Don't worry, Lorraine. Whatever you tell me is in strict confidence. Unless you're thinking of hurting yourself in some way. That I have to report immediately."

"No, nothing like that. I was just wondering…"

"Yes…?"

"Well, if adultery with a married guy is bad —"

"It is."

"I know. But if adultery with a married man is bad, is adultery with someone in a covenant marriage illegal?"

"Illegal?"

"I know you're not supposed to sleep with anyone who's already hooked up. But is it against the law to sleep with someone in a covenant marriage?

"No," Tom was paying attention now. "It's not."

"Whew! But it's morally worse than cheating with a regular guy, right?"

"They're both wrong. Lorraine, is there something you should be telling me?" The teenager looked down into her very ample bosoms. "If you're in trouble, I can try to help," he added. "But you have to tell me what's going on."

Lorraine thought for a moment, and then decided it was time to come clean.

"Do you know who Derek Chase is?"

"Yes."

"Well…I may have sort of fucked him."

Tom almost choked on his own tongue.

Lorraine looked up at him with moist eyes. "Am I in trouble?"

❖ ❖ ❖ ❖ ❖

Jeff Joseph was sitting in his office, squeezing in a few extra moments of rolling calls before his next meeting with a screenwriter who said she had the perfect vehicle for Myra's next project. What Jeff didn't know when his assistant booked the meeting is that the writer was coming in to pitch a period piece in which Myra would play an

1880s hooker in a frontier western saloon. No way was he going to put Myra Dreyer — one of the hottest bodies in Hollywood — into a period piece with her covered in frumpy old west dresses and ugly-ass corsets. Jeff didn't cancel the meeting because the writer was coming off a blockbuster hit action film with Miley Cyrus as a Russian Cosmonaut who saves America from an intergalactic terrorist attack. Maybe she had an idea like that for Myra.

While rolling calls, Jeff was flipping through the latest *American Peephole* to see what the masses were reading about. On page three he came across a piece that caught his attention – something about a course in murder taught by Helen Fay Crittenden. *Now that is a movie!* he thought. *Famous female murderer beats the rap and then teaches others how to kill their spouse. Genius. Maybe I'll pitch that to this writer for Aniston or Lopez.*

As Jeff considered the idea, he was struck by how smart Helen Crittenden had been to teach a class like that. Now THAT is publicity. Someone writes an article like this about it in *The Peephole* and her best selling book, which has dwindled in sales in the years since it was published, starts flying off the shelves again. *Smart cookie, this*

Crittenden. Jeff admired the way she branded herself after the trial with the books and a line of Helen Fay Crittenden signature claw hammers with the blood-red hammer heads. *Maybe there's something here.*

What Jeff was considering was possibly signing the celebrated murderess and see if her brand could be packaged into movies, TV series, books, and even merchandize. *Maybe pair her with the writer of the piece and see what they can come up with.* Jeff scanned back to the top and looked at the article's byline.

Ken Feldman. That asshole? Okay, well that's not gonna happen. Jeff hated Ken, even though he knew his *Peephole* pieces were great for his clients. The problem with guys like Ken Feldman, in Jeff's mind, was that they think they're journalists. So while they may be trying to sell magazines and help promote our people, they occasionally came across a real news story and dig too deep. And the last thing a major talent agency wants is for reporters to be looking for and printing real news about their clients. Like that "You Lost Me Between the Sheets" hit piece he had written about Ian and Myra. That one piece had probably cost her over ten million in movie fees, meaning nearly a million out of Jeff's pocket. So, no, Ken Feldman was not going to be pitching film ideas in Jeff's office or anywhere in his agency. Not in this lifetime.

But Helen Fay Crittenden, she's another story.

"Adrian!" Jeff bellowed to his desk assistant sitting just outside his office. "Find a number for Helen Fay Crittenden and see if you can roll her into my next set of calls."

"Crittenden? Who is she with?"

"She's not 'with' anyone, num-nuts. She's the rich chick who bashed her husband's head in and got away with it. Get her for me."

"Any idea who to call?"

Jeff scanned the article again. "Try a company called *Dinnertime University* in L.A."

"On it!"

Jeff would never end up signing Helen or doing business with her. On their call when he tried to dig for details on the murder, he found her evasive and abrasive about whether she had actually done the dirty deed or not. Jeff was so cocky about his super agent standing that he expected the world's most celebrated murder suspect to give him the confession that had eluded every police detective and prosecutor.

But Jeff did remember the article, and the name of the company that had sponsored her class. *Dinnertime University,* which offered Adult Ed classes on any and every topic in the world. *Hm. Maybe there's a Netflix sitcom in that.*

Lisa Prococino was in the shower when her cell phone rang. Normally Lisa wouldn't climb out of her morning shower to take a call. But today was not going to be a normal day. No day is normal when you stand to earn two million dollars.

Lisa had grown up in a small suburb of Atlanta, Georgia called Peachtree City, a two-horse southern town forty miles south of Atlanta that was converted in the late fifties into a series of planned subdivisions of stately brick houses on one acre lots. Like most suburban sprawl of the twentieth century, it's development was guided by greed and not sound community planning. Subdivisions bloomed around the center of the tiny town like malignant tumors, each one taking a parcel of beautiful farm country and turning it into a maze of suburban streets and cul-de-sacs. Without a town or an industry to support it, the city may have fallen into hard times.

But as luck would have it, the airline industry conspired to help out. Hartsfield-Jackson International Airport in Atlanta became one of the major hubs of the airline industry in the 1970s, and Delta Airlines chose it as its main southeastern hub for the United States, the Caribbean and Latin America. That brought pilots and flight attendants to live near there – many from Northeast and Mid-Western cities like New York and Chicago. And most of them chose to make one of the new, stately subdivisions of Peachtree City their home, quickly morphing PTC into one of the most culturally diverse and highly educated towns outside Atlanta.

Lisa's father had been one of those pilots. After twenty-one years on the job, he took early retirement to go off and form his own private charter airline that made him a fortune. Now in his eighties, Jim Prococino had long left Georgia for a real retirement in Bel Air, California. A retirement that was going swimmingly except for one thing: his red-headed fourth daughter. Lisa had been a trouble-maker as a youth and by Jim's estimate, hadn't matured much since then. A bright, handsome girl, she glided through college to emerge with good grades and a B.A. in Abnormal Psychology but no discernible marketable skills to live on. And even less in the way of ambition.

What Lisa lived on was other men's money. First, her dad's. Then wealthy boyfriends. Then a not-so-wealthy husband from a short-lived marriage that saw him rip her off to the tune of fifty-thousand dollars. Then her father again. Then a series of guy pals and fuck buddies who would let her crash until they found her "palling around" with someone else. Most of those relationships ended with her getting kicked to the curb. One ended in that plus an abortion, paid for by her parents. Whereas her three sisters and one brother had either gone to work, married, raised families, or all three, Lisa was the family dilettante and black sheep. An avid reader, she consumed books by the dozens, mostly trashy novels and salacious non-fiction, but had no interest in the grunt work of making a living in the real world. By thirty, she had lived off her looks and her parents beyond all reasonable parameters, without ever bothering to look for a job or choose a profession.

Her parents did the only thing they could think of to help their second-youngest daughter finally grow up: they cut off the cash spigot.

That didn't sit well with Lisa. But the ever creative, ever plotting Lisa Prococino always had a plan of action. Whereas in the past her schemes were based on a trickle-down economy mindset of living off the breadcrumbs of other people, her latest plan would finally establish her own independent wealth. One day while perusing the business section of her favorite Barnes & Noble, Lisa skimmed a few chapters of a personal finance book that explained the concept of annuities, and how a smart investor could layer her returns over the years with annuities that paid off at different intervals.

However, to invest in annuities, you needed money. And Lisa had little of that. What she did have plenty of were relatives – parents and siblings of various ages who would not live forever. Growing up, Lisa had seen her grandmother, two aunts and three classmate friends all die prematurely, most by unexpected illness and two by unexpected car fenders. Plus, her oldest brother, Larry, a pilot for her dad's private transport company, died in a twin-engine plane crash that also killed four passengers. The NTSB investigation found serious flaws in the mechanical upkeep of the downed aircraft, and the legal and emotional blowback decimated the Prococino family for years. As an adult Lisa would learn that her dad had made it a practice to take out life insurance policies on his company's pilots, and had profited handsomely from his oldest son's untimely demise. Lisa had learned the hard way that life is fleeting and the only sure bet is on death. And often, premature death.

So Lisa invested in life insurance policies. Using some illegitimate means (including her parents' credit cards), Lisa was able to purchase a series of laddered term life policies on her parents and four surviving siblings. By her math, the odds were in her favor to hit on at least one in the next ten years. *Who knows,* she thought. *Maybe I'll hit a double or trifecta! Then I'm set for life.*

But today it seemed her morbid calculations may have been too conservative. At three in the morning, Lisa had been awakened by a call saying her second oldest sister, Connie, had been rushed to the hospital with a massive stroke and was in critical condition. Lisa was so excited she could barely get back to sleep. And during her morning shower she was fantasizing about how she would spend the two million dollar payout if Connie succumbed.

When her phone rang, she grabbed a towel and made a beeline for it.

"Hello!"

"Hi. Is this Lisa Prococino?"

"Why, yes it is," she said with a chirp in her voice. She had learned from Helen Fey Crittenden to always seem upbeat when speaking to authorities. Tentative, defensive people sound guilty.

"This is Ken Feldman. From *The American Peephole.*"

A reporter, she thought excitedly. *Maybe he's calling to break the bad news!*

"You may remember me from the *Dinnertime University* class we took together last winter?"

Lisa was thrown. "Uh, yeah, Ken...I think I remember you." She didn't.

"Good, good. But this isn't a social call. I'm calling for *The Peephole.* I'm trying to track down one of our fellow classmates. Jerry Proud. I kinda noticed you two seemed to become friendly outside of class and I thought maybe you had a contact number for him?"

This wasn't the call Lisa wanted, nor the way she wanted to start her day. Jerry Proud was a bad memory of a poor decision – a night when she let a rush of adrenaline from the role-playing exercise lead her to a regretful roll in the hay. Now some reporter was linking her to him. And with a loser like Jerry Proud, nothing good could come of that.

"Uh, yeah, Ken. I may still have his number. But I'm not sure I should be giving it out to strangers."

"Well, I'm not a stranger. We all took the class together."

"I'm not sure I feel comfortable."

"Understood, understood. I'll tell you what. Do you think you could get my number to him? You'd be doing me and him both a solid."

"Um, look, I jumped out of the shower to get this and I'm expecting a very important call. I have your number now. Let me think about it and decide how to proceed. Is that okay?"

"Fair enough," Ken said. Then, trying to solidify their connection, Ken ventured into lighter territory. "Man, that class was crazy, wasn't it?"

"Uh, yeah, guess so."

"Who do you think it was?"

"Who do I think what was?

"The killer? I figure in a class like that, at least one nut had to take it with the thought of real murder on their mind. Who do you think? My money is on the tight-assed rich lady from Beverly Hills. Fiona something? Man, I wouldn't sleep at night being her husband." Ken added a light laugh to show he was joking.

"Hey Ken, I hate to be rude, but I got a call coming in. Gotta run." Before he could respond, she had clicked him away.

"Hello?"

"Hey Leese, it's Chelle. Good news, Mavis is awake and out of ICU. You wanna say hi to her?"

"Huh? No. She probably needs to rest. Just tell her I send my best. Thanks for the update."

"Hey, when are you gonna fly out to see—"

Lisa clicked her off, then popped an Ativan. *What a fucking shitty way to start the day!*

Tom Reiner and Sandy Yoeste didn't speak for the rest of the month. Oh, sure, he'd acknowledge her politely if they passed in the hallways and she'd be courteous to him in the faculty lounge. But as far as small talk, they both steered clear of each other.

Unbeknownst to both of them was the fact that their awkward Macaroni Grill dinner had set off a domino effect of events from Hollywood to New York. that would change much of American life.

After the meal, Sandy went home and called

her brother Bobby, who worked in the Media and Publicity Department at Paramount. They hadn't talked in a few weeks and Bobby was pleased to hear from his little sister, and she told him about an English teacher named Dominick who had recently invited her to the opera. But since they were coworkers, Sandy was still weighing whether she should accept the invitation or not.

His sister seemed genuinely excited by this new prospect, though, and Bobby was happy about that. People in Hollywood work together and date all the time. He didn't see what the big fuss was about. "After all, work is where you spend eighty percent of your waking hours," he counseled his baby sister. "If you aren't allowed to date the people you meet there, you might as well stop your hands from cutting your food because your hands work with your mouth." Sandy didn't really get that analogy but she thanked her big brother for the dating advice.

When she asked him about knowing Derek or Myra and told him about Mr. Reiner's idea, Bobby was intrigued enough to say he'd make some calls and see what comes back.

The next day, Bobby told his supervisor about the conversation, which started a telephone game throughout Hollywood and New York from publicity departments to agents to managers, back to publicity departments and finally to the phone of Jeff Josephs at Galaxy Talent, who loved the idea.

Because what Josephs knew that the rest of the world didn't, was that Derek had recently been caught cheating with some 16-year old piece of ass, which Myra got wind of and confronted him about. During the heated argument, Myra threatened to go public with the photos of Derek and the 16-year old blonde if he didn't pay her off to the tune of $50,000,000 and a commit to a total news blackout on her own "comings and goings" for the rest of their covenant marriage. Absent that, she threatened, she would get the horrifyingly graphic sex photos out there and unleash the financial hounds of hell on him for breaking their covenant.

Naturally, Derek was boiling mad – not just at the blackmail threat, but also that she had apparently spied on him with Lorraine and maybe had even set him up. But Derek had some aces up his own sleeve as well. He went into his home office and quickly reappeared with a handful of photos of his own– shots of Myra and Ian banging in toilet stalls and TV greenrooms that were just as raw and embarrassing as the Lorraine shots. Myra protested; she hadn't slept with Ian since before the second wedding when she and Derek were broken up. Those photos were from back then – an affair the entire world already knew about.

"Says you," Derek calmly tossed back.

"What do you mean?" Myra grew enraged. Only Derek knew just how enraged she could get. It was a well-kept secret in Hollywood that Myra had a temper, but her close friends (all two of them) knew her anger management issues well.

"Last year, this year…who's gonna know the difference but you and Ian. To the rest of the world these images will be fresh. And if I say my P.I. took them last month, who's gonna believe a lying slut like you?"

Myra slapped him, hard. He smiled, knowing that would enrage her even more. It did. She hit him again, this time with a closed fist, and it packed a wallop. But Derek had been in some street fights of his own when he was a teen and could take a pretty good punch.

"You hit me," he said, using the best of his acting training to look surprised and emotionally hurt. He even managed to produce a tear on cue. No one ever said Derek wasn't a fine actor.

"Yeah, and if you don't give me those photos

right this fucking second, Derek, I'll get a knife from the kitchen and show you how I really feel."

Derek was used to his wife's bipolar violent outbursts. And he played her like a fine violin.

"Yeah, what're you gonna do, kill me, Myra?"

"No, just cut your limp dick balls off. Don't fuck with me, D. I know people who know people. My dad knows people. People who DO kill pieces of shit like you. Gimme those photos, Derek. You're not leaving this house until I have them and the masters."

Derek smiled a very satisfied grin. "Fine. Here." He calmly offered up the snapshots to her. She ripped them to shreds.

"And the masters."

"Sure, no prob, I'll have my P.I. send them to you from his safe. Oh, and you're probably want a copy of this, too."

On that, Derek slid his cellphone out of his shirt breast pocket. What Myra hadn't noticed when Derek came back from his office was that he had turned on the video camera on his phone and placed it inconspicuously in his pocket, lens pointing out, so he could record the violent event he was pretty sure was in the making. He did a very quick, deft

edit of the footage on his camera app, deleting the
first few lines that might have explained Myra's ire,
and sent her a copy of what was left: Myra blowing
up at Derek over some photos of her, slapping him,
punching him, threatening him with a knife, and
threatening to have him killed by a hired hit man.

Myra's phone dinged and she watched the 42
second video he'd just texted her. Her jaw dropped.
In her haste to blackmail Derek, she had walked
into a trap of his own. Now *he* had the goods on
her!

Myra was apoplectic, ranting and throwing
things until there was little left to break. Derek just
let her seethe. By the end of the night they had both
called their agents and entertainment attorneys to
tell their side of what had transpired.

The agents and attorneys were quickly on the
phone with each other, jockeying and threatening
and strategizing their way out of this client-made
clusterfuck of a mess. What they settled on after a
few days of wrangling and angry recriminations was
that neither party would go public with their
respective photos, and no one would be filing for
divorce. This situation had come up many times in
old Hollywood, often between straight actresses and
their closeted gay movie star husbands. The

marriage would remain intact – the parties would maintain the public aura of a happy couple – and they could live in separate domiciles and bang anyone they wanted to. Myra could have Ian on the side. (He didn't want a full-blown committed relationship with her, anyway.) Derek could bang anyone he wanted. (Though he was strongly and loudly counseled by his reps that any more jailbait incidents would lead to them dropping him for good.)

In return for his jailbait discretion, Derek agreed to donate a half million dollars into a college fund for future film students. Quite a bargain against the fifty mil Myra was angling for.

The "Derek and Myra Chase Film Scholarship," as they eventually named it, pledged to help fund college educations for deserving high school students who were hoping to make their own contribution to the cinematic arts. Lorraine Leaver just happened to be its first recipient.

To the tune of $250 grand.

Jerry Proud was jerking off in the shower when he heard his cell phone ringing. Needing time to rinse and dry off, he didn't get there before the call went dead. But when he saw his home screen, the caller ID couldn't have been more surprising. It had been from Lisa Prococino. Jerry quickly dialed her back.

"Lisa?"

"Yeah, hi, Jerry."

"Hey, long time, no see. I've been thinking about you. How ya doing?"

"Good, Jerry, good. But I only have a second to chat."

"Oh. Okay. What's up?"

"Well, I just thought you should know – remember that class we took together?"

"Of course I remember. It was only four months ago."

"Right. Remember the skinny, nerdy guy who always sat way in the back and didn't talk a lot? The reporter guy? Ken Feldman?"

"Yeah, I think so."

"Well, he remembers you."

"What do you mean?"

"He somehow got my number and he called me today, asking if I had a contact number for you. I didn't give it to him. I really try to honor people's privacy. But he was asking about you and I got the sense he'd been looking for you so I figured you might want to know."

"Wow, Lisa, that's nice. I really appreciate it. Do you have his number? Maybe I should find out why he's looking for me."

"Uh, yeah, let me look it up in my recents. Here it is." Lisa reeled off the ten digit phone number.

"Did you get the sense I was in some kind of trouble or anything? I mean, a reporter..."

"Yeah. No, I didn't get the sense that he was angry or anything. Maybe he's just doing a piece on the class and he wants to interview you."

"Did he interview you?"

"No, not really. Just about you. He wanted to know if I remembered you and knew anything about you, like your occupation and stuff. I said I didn't really know you that well. Then he asked if I knew anything about you being in the computer security business. Of course, I know what you do – you told me that night we...y'know. But I didn't say anything to him about it. I figured, if it's information he wants about you, you should be the one who decides to give it to him or not."

"Good instincts. I always thought your were pretty bright."

"Yeah. Well, I gotta go. That's really all I had

to say."

"Really? Cause I'd love to catch up."

"Yeah, well, I'm late to dinner with my boyfriend."

"Boyfriend?"

"Yeah, nice guy. I met him at a bookstore a few weeks ago, and things just fell into place. Know what I mean?"

"Yeah. Sure. I'm happy for you."

"Thanks. Anyhoo. I gotta run. Good luck with this Ken Feldman thing. I hope it's nothing bad."

"Thanks, Lisa. And good luck with this new —" The line went dead. Bitch!

Once he was toweled off and dressed, Jerry called Ken Feldman to ask why he was looking for him. Feldman said he recalled Jerry mentioning something about being in the cybersecurity field, and his newspaper was looking for an indy contractor to take on an assignment in that area.

Jerry listened to Ken's pitch and was intrigued by the challenge. He hadn't really done any hacking since college but his job required him to keep up on the latest in business cybersecurity, and he had a pretty good idea of where each software system's weak spots were and how to navigate around them. When Ken told him the targets, Jerry perked up.

"Marquee7? Shit, I sold to those guys. I know exactly what programs they're using and what backdoors they leave open."

"So you think you can get into their servers?"

"It's not a question of servers. All you need is to get access to the right laptop's hard drive. If they ever saved the document there, it'll still be there, even if they tried to erase it. And most people who use word processing software save each file at least a few times as they're working in it, just in case their computer crashes. If you can get me the names of the people you think may have touched the document and their email addresses, odds are one of them will hand us this buried treasure and never even know about it."

"Impressive. How much would it cost me?"

Jerry knew that The American Peephole was a big international company with deep pockets so he decided to shoot for the fences.

"Fifteen hundred dollars." Jerry heard silence on the other end. Then...

"Can you do it for seven-hundred-fifty?"

"Deal!"

Lisa Proud had no idea what her husband was working on, but she had not seen him so fixated on his work in years. Jerry sat at his laptop all day and well into the night working on something that delighted him. She asked what it was all about, but he barely grunted an answer.

"My project. My details."

As Lisa bathed the kids, put them down and then hit the sheets herself, Jerry was chugging coffee and typing on his Dell well into the night. When she woke up in the morning, she could tell he had come to bed at some point in the night. But he was already up and back in his lime green office and at it again. This went on for three days.

Then on the morning of day four, a Saturday, she woke up to the whir of their ink jet printer spitting out page after page. She went to check on Jerry and found him standing by the printer reading pages and pages of dense text, ecstatic at what he was reading.

"What is that?"

"The worst fucking contract in the history of mankind."

"Huh?"

"Honey, if you thought our covenant marriage had strict rules, you don't know the meaning of the word strict."

"Jerry, are you in trouble of some kind?

Jerry laughed.

"No baby. But I'm gonna make some for lots of assholes who deserve it."

Myra and Derek were seated on the couch in Jeff Joseph's office as Jeff read them the riot act while calling them every form of "stupid" in the English language.

"How do you idiots even think? Do you wake up and take moron pills, then go to the simpleton gym and do cretin exercises?"

"We get the point," Derek said, half ashamed of himself.

"No, I don't think you do. You got married the first time, and I told you both you were too young. " Then turning to Derek, "Then YOU take a gig in the Philippines and hand her over to the most lecherous man on the planet for safe keeping. " Then to Myra, "Then YOU fuck said lecherous man till he gets tired of you cumming on his dick. Then he dumps you, which of course any halfwit bimbo in the world would see coming—"

"Hey!" Derek blurted meekly.

"Then you go back to dickforbrains for a second marriage – again ignoring my advice – and YOU," eying Derek, "…proceed to fuck a complete stranger that sexted you out of nowhere and don't even check her age first? I mean, are you looking to go to prison forever? Because that's what the 'jail' in jailbait means, Derek. Jail. As in maximum security prison."

"Okay, he knows he screwed up. Now what?" Myra was getting heated.

"He screwed up? You both screwed up! And as always, now me and a lot of expensive attorneys have to wipe your asses and clean up your mess again. So this is what you're going to do. Not only are you going to pay me each a million dollars–"

"What?"

"Shut up, Derek! Not only are you each gonna happily give me a million bucks in cash. But you're going to do every publicity event I ask of you and every junket a studio asks of you, and you're going to hold hands in public and steal kisses in public and fuck in public if I tell you to. With the shit in those photos and the threats you made on that video, you could be in the hole to this agency for money you'll never come close to earning for the rest of your fucking, miserable sexpot lives. If I tell you to show up in Kansas City and do a circus act with a syphilitic elephant, you'll do it. Understood?"

The two biggest stars of their generation nodded and bowed their heads like abused puppies.

"Good, but I don't believe you for a second. So we're going to test your newly pledged fealty to us a few weeks from now. You ever heard of *Dinnertime University*?"

"Uh... I don't think so."

"Well, you're about to. Morons!"

Tom Reiner picked up the new *Dinnertime University* catalog, hoping to see that they had re-scheduled his course on covenant marriages. What he found shocked him.

Yes, there was a new course featured on the cover about covenant marriages. But it wasn't his. It was something called "Covenant Kingdom: Make Your Marriage Happily Ever After," a one-day seminar about super vow marriages featuring happily married movie stars Derek Chase and Myra Dreyer.

How could this be, Tom seethed. That was MY idea!

What had happened was, Jeff Josephs had decided his newly remarried client's film career was on the rocks and she needed a quick dose of positive PR to get the offers rolling in again. That happened just as the Hollywood game of telephone that Bobby Yoeste had started about Derek and Myra doing a *Dinnertime University* course about their marriage had come to Jeff's attention. Jeff had been intrigued when he'd learned about Helen Fay Crittenden's course and the media coverage it had garnered, and he thought this might be the perfect shlock idea to help rebrand his client.

So he called up *Dinnertime U* and pitched the idea for a "course" that could be promoted as a huge event, with the happy couple regaling the world in stories about the romantic bliss of their second, covenant marriage.

Of course, the *Dinnertime U* folks jumped at the offer. Knowing this could be a major event for them, they decided to forgo a classroom setting and hold the seminar outdoors in their large courtyard, where they could pack the "students" in. *Dinnertime* offered the one-day "class" for $99 (plus registration fees), and within days of the catalog's release they had sold over 2,000 tickets. So they ditched their first setting and got a permit to use

Griffith Park, one of the largest open spaces in Los Angeles. They would stage the event like a mock wedding and have it "catered" by food trucks (with the *University* taking a cut). Of course, they agreed to list Jeff Josephs as the "producer" of the event, so he could nab his greedy cut. And Derek and Myra agreed (per Jeff's insistence) on donating their end to the newly established Derek and Myra Chase Film Scholarship Fund. Jeff figured that having them do the event for charity (and plugging the name, "Derek and Myra Chase") would help their PR story and add to the upbeat, storybook feel of the whole affair.

Tom Reiner was furious. This was MY idea, he fumed to himself. But nowhere in the course blurb was he mentioned. Within minutes Tom was on the phone to the school's "worldwide headquarters" in Lancaster, the armpit of Southern California's Antelope Valley.

"*Dinnertime University*. Hope you're having a great day! How can I help you?"

"You can help me by not stealing my course."

"Excuse me?"

Tom went on to explain to the very confused receptionist that he had been scheduled to teach a course on covenant marriages, which had been cancelled due to low enrollment. But now they were offering a similar course starring Derek and Myra. And that he had had the exact same idea for his next course and had even told it to a few friends. ("Few" being exactly one: Sandra Yoeste.)

After being put on hold for fifteen minutes and transferred a few times around the small office, Tom found himself reexplaining his situation to a fellow named Eduardo, who had identified himself as the Assistant to the Registrar. Eduardo patiently listened as Tom railed about how unfair this all was and how he was going to sue *Dinnertime U* if the didn't "make things right" with him.

Eduardo, whose minimum wage job mostly consisted of taking class registrations and proofing the catalog for typos, calmly apologized to Tom for the miscommunication but assured him that the school had not "stolen" the idea from him. Eduardo explained how Myra's agent had contacted his boss. Even though the seminar shared the same subject matter as Tom's class, it was just a sad coincidence. And they would be happy to offer his class again at some unspecified future date.

"Oh, yeah, right. Who's gonna sign up for my class after you have two movie starts teaching this one?"

"Actually, sir, I think this could generate more interest in your course. They will be promoting the positive aspects of covenant marriages. Your class teaches people how to go about it. You see? They have synergy together. To your advantage."

"Don't 'synergy' me. You'll probably sell hundreds of tickets to theirs, and I'll be lucky to get a dozen signups."

Eduardo didn't bother to tell Tom that he'd underestimated the numbers. The Myra-Derek course had already sold almost 3,500 tickets and demand was still strong. Instead, he put Tom on hold for another ten minutes while he relayed the problem to his boss. For a minimum wage employee, Eduardo was on top of things, courteous, and in control. He came back on the phone with the perfect tone.

"Mr. Raynor – did I pronounce that right?"

"Rye-ner, yeah."

"Mr. Reiner, I communicated your matter to our Chancellor of Education and he fully sympathizes with your concerns. And we do want to make things right. So even though this was entirely an unintentional coincidence, we are going to pay you the full $100 instructor's fee for the seminar, and you won't even have to teach it."

Tom wasn't born yesterday. He knew they were offering him the "instructor's fee" so he couldn't later sue them for plagiarizing his idea. But that Macaroni Grill dinner for two had set him back a bit, so he was grateful for the newfound revenue stream.

"Plus..." Eduardo continued, "...we will make sure the emcee at the event mentions your upcoming course, which will certainly grab a lot of attention for it."

Tom was somewhat placated. "Yeah, well... that's something."

"And..." Eduardo moved in for the kill, "... we will also be glad to send you a free ticket to the seminar so you can be there to promote your course yourself, if you like. I understand that several of our instructors are setting up booths there. You can pass out flyers and even start an informal waitlist that we can use once your class has been rescheduled. So, you see, this can really work out great for you. For your class, I mean."

"And I get paid the whole hundred bucks?"

"Yes sir. I'll mail the check myself. Does that sound fair?

Tom figured he was still getting the short end of the stick somehow. But a hundred bucks was a hundred bucks.

"Fine."

"Great."

"But I want your promise that my class will be offered next quarter."

"Well, our Spring catalog has already gone to print. But I will remind the Chancellor of our conversation and make sure he knows about you and your course idea."

"Maybe they could introduce me onstage—"

"Oh, I'm sorry, the phones are ringing off the hook. I'll get that paycheck and ticket out to you asap. Have a great day!" Click.

Tom looked at his phone. *Ah, what the hell. 'Least I got something.*

Eduardo looked at his phone. No other lines were ringing.

Ken Feldman was at his desk at *The Peephole* when a text came across his phone from a number he didn't recognize.

"I've got some dirt on Derek Chase you may be interested in, scumbag."

Quite a unique opening approach, Ken thought. He got lots of tips from lots of crazies, and lots of derisive threats from lots of crazies. But he rarely got tips and derision in the same sentence.

"Who is this" he thumb typed back.

"Never mind who I am, dickwad. How much would it be worth to The American Peepshow to learn about a certain male movie star who was screwing around with an underage high school kid?" Ken noted that they misspelled "Peephole." He was not dealing with a particularly bright person.

"We don't do that kind of 'journalism' here."

"Oh please. Who do you think you're dealing with?"

"I don't know. You won't tell me." Ken was kind of proud of that line.

"Either you want the story, or I go to the Enquirer. Either way, the truth is going to get out. It's just a matter of who tells it. You, or your competitors."

"Let me check with my managing editor," Ken typed back, *"and let you know what we can do."*

Ken was more than aware that *The Peephole* sometimes paid for big stories; he often delivered the checks. But he also knew that they were there to promote movie star's careers, not destroy them.

Ken ran the details of the text thread past his managing editor, who ran it past the editor-in-chief, who ran it past the lawyers, who ran it past the police and FBI, who wanted to set up a meeting with the texter and wire Ken, who adamantly refused to wear a wire, whose boss then said, "Fuck it, if this guy has a real story, let's see what it's worth and go from there."

"Okay, my bosses are willing to consider some financial renumeration for this story... IF it's solid and IF you have proof to back it up. It's gotta be rock solid."

Tom read the text reply and considered his options. Lorraine was a good girl – a poor student and a bit of a slut, but a nice kid nonetheless. He didn't want to see her hurt. He also knew that because she was a minor, he was bound to report what she had told him, a criminal felony against a student, to his principle. But Tom knew that nothing good would come of reporting it to Mrs. Angler, who would immediately report it to the police. That would just create a torrid he said/she said complaint that would probably end up hurting the victim, Lorraine, more than the adult who had taken advantage of her. He had asked Lorraine directly if she wanted to go to the police with the complaint, and her answer was an adamant 'no.' She didn't want her parents to find out and she didn't want to get Derek in any trouble. And she didn't want to risk losing the surprise scholarship she had "won." She just wanted to make sure SHE hadn't committed any crime, and Tom disabused her of that mistaken notion.

But Tom was still worried. What if she continues the affair, and things get worse for her. What if she gets pregnant, like Alicia Strandquest? A slime-ball like this Derek Chase character would surely bail on her, and Lorraine would become another sad statistic of unwanted high school pregnancy. Like Alicia.

BUT...

But if Tom could figure out some way to capitalize on Derek's abominable behavior, he could get something out of it for Lorraine. (She hadn't told him about the 'film scholarship.') And maybe something for Tom's time and righteous concerns, as well.

Now the only question was, how could Tom play this with only Lorraine's version of events and no Lorraine to back it up?

"Tell me, what does a story like this pay IF YOU CAN VERIFY THAT IT'S TRUE?

"I can't tell you for sure. That would be up to my bosses," Ken typed back with his editor-in-chief and two lawyers looking over his shoulder. *"But I can tell you that the most we've ever paid for a story is $5,000."* That was not true; *The Peephole* had paid up to twenty-five grand for major stories like exclusive rights to the first Myra-Derek wedding. But this was not a story that was going to sell nearly as many copies, and frankly they didn't plan to go much above twenty-five hundred for this tip, even if it was golden.

"Five grand will do."

"I didn't say you'd get five thousand. I said that's the highest we've ever gone. You won't get that much."

"Put it this way," Tom typed back. *"You've been informed that a 16-year old girl was raped by a star you cover repeatedly in your paper. That is a felony, and covering it up is aiding and abetting a felony. So if you reject this story, you may be opening your paper up to some serious legal jeopardy for covering up a statutory rape? How much would defending against THAT cost you?"*

Ken couldn't believe how stupid some of the

general public could be. This idiot just tried to extort five thousand dollars from a newspaper and texted the threat from his own cellphone.

Guess who's in legal jeopardy now, Ken thought with a smile.

While Ken, his bosses and lawyers, and Tom were haggling over price, Ken spotted a new voice mail on his phone from Jerry Proud.

"Ken, this is Jerry. Good news. I was able to find a copy of the document. The bad news is, it's heavily redacted. But what's there should be more than enough to write your story. I'll drop it off tomorrow. Please have the check for seven-fifty ready for me."

Ken was confused; why would an internal document from a talent agency be redacted?

His instinct was right. Jerry's hacked copy was clean and complete. But Jerry, ever the con artist, had decided to redact the juiciest tidbits and keep them for himself to possibly blackmail Derek or Myra or their agents...or all of them. Hey, he had found the document, which is what *The Peephole* hired him to do, he reasoned. And nothing in the deal said anything about redactions. So the next day,

Jerry swung by Ken's office with the redacted covenant contract.

Ken and his managing editor were disappointed by all the large black rectangles of redacted sections. But by now they were more intrigued with the jailbait angle of the Derek story, so they decided to just pay Proud off and be done with him.

Jerry was delighted with his hefty payday, taking several cellphone photos of the check before cashing it.

Then he placed a call to a guy whose name he had heard in passing as Ken and his bosses were discussing the story: Jeff Josephs. Jerry had seen that name on the email to which the document was attached.

This guy Josephs must be tight with Myra and Derek, he figured. *Let's see if I can squeeze him and get him to play ball.*

◆ ◆ ◆ ◆ ◆

"Jeff, call for you on line three," Adrian called from his desk.

"Who?"

"Some guy named Jerry. Won't give his last name. But he says you'd better pick up or his next call is to the police."

"The police? About what?"

"Damned if I know. He sounds kinda wired or something."

"Okay, put him through." Jeff composed himself as the line three button began to blink. He picked up.

"This is Jeff Josephs."

"Okay, I'm not gonna waste a lot of time here. I got a document that you probably don't want me to have. And you definitely don't want the newspapers to have."

"Who is this," Jeff interacted, trying to take back control of the conversation.

"Yeah, like I'm gonna give you my name. Want my social security number as well? Come on, I'm not playin' around here."

"I don't even know what you're talking about. What document?"

"Let's just say it's got the name of one of your biggest female stars on it and it contains a lot of info about her marriage that I'm pretty sure you don't want public."

"The covenant contract?"

"All twenty-eight pages."

Jeff noted that the guy had the right page

count. Which meant he probably had the actual document. "*Shit!*"

"However you got whatever it is you think you have, you should not be in possession of it. That could get you in a world of trouble. So why don't you mail it to me and destroy any copies you have, and we'll forget this conversation ever–"

"Don't get stupid on me now, Josephs. Fifty-grand gets me to destroy this thing and make sure it never sees the light of day. While you think about it, let me read you one of my favorite sections: Paragraph 22.d. 'The parties to this contract hereby indemnify Galaxy Talent Agency, Inc. and Marquee7 International Enterprises from any future loss of income due to any breach of this contract and the covenants of marriage herein up to 80% of all their future earnings from any source, including acting fees, writing fees, producing fees, directing fees, packaging fees, speaking fees–"

"Okay, okay." Jeff hated hearing the incredibly coercive language of the contract read out loud. He knew it would't play any better coming out of the mouth of some TV reporter. "Look, I understand what you want. But you have to understand, this is a publicly traded company. Our books are audited constantly. And we don't have a budget line for paying off bribes and ransom."

"Oh, like you guys can't afford it?"

"I didn't say we can't afford it. I said, we can't pay it. I'd be committing an S.E.C. felony."

"Then get your stars to pay it. Shit, they probably got a hundred times that much in wedding gifts alone."

Jeff realized he had an amateur on the line, so he decided to back up and think this through. "Okay, give me your number and I'll see what–"

"No no no, I'm not giving you any numbers. You think I'm dumb? You think I'm stupid? This is a burner phone, but I gotta ditch it the minute this call is over. And buy a new one for every call I make to you. Which is $30 outta my pocket." *My god, this putz really is smalltime. I give the mailroom kid a $30 dollar tip just to take my car to be detailed. And he's complaining about thirty bucks against a fifty grand demand?!"*

"I'll give you twenty-four hours," the blackmailer continued. "Be ready to take my call at exactly three p.m. tomorrow. And Mr. Josephs," Jerry said with emphasis, "that is gonna be the last chance you have to buy this document back. My next call after that: CNN." The line went dead.

◆ ◆ ◆ ◆ ◆

Back at Ken's office, they were perusing a photo of Derek Chase naked, with his hand almost touching his junk. The day before at Downey High School, Tom had called Lorraine back into his office and told her he needed a copy of the text thread and the photos "for his records." Lorraine, being all of sixteen with cognitive functions of a first year Girl Scout, obliged his request.

Ken was now starting to believe the guy on the other end of this text string might actually have the goods. The screenshots of the texts he sent looked authentic, and a quick check of his Rolodex showed that one of the phone numbers did indeed belong to Derek Chase. Of course, anyone could've doctored the screen grab to add that phone number. But they'd have to *know* Derek's cellphone number, and the number of people who had that must be fairly small.

Could this be Ian trying to get his ex-friend in trouble? Or a former girlfriend who was pissed he'd ditched her?

Ken realized he had to assume this extortionist was for real. And he knew his bosses would never publish a story that might send one of the biggest box office stars in the world to prison. So he did the most honorable thing he could think to do in the moment.

"Hey, Derek, this is Ken Feldman. I got something really important to talk to you about. Are you alone?"

Needless to say, Derek freaked out. First Myra tried to blackmail him. Now some idiot had the story and was trying to get his payday. Though the five thousand bribe amount Ken had mentioned was a far cry from the fifty million Myra wanted. Derek needed to focus and *think.*

"Ken, first of all, thanks buddy for bringing this to my attention. I'm sure I don't have to say it, but I want you to know, the jailbait part of the story is not true. I get weird offers and sext texts like that all the time. You wouldn't believe some of the shit people send me."

"Oh, I believe it."

"And I'm not saying I've always been a choir boy. But a sixteen year-old? No fucking way." Derek added the curse word to make it sound authentic.

"Derek, I'm not here passing judgment."

"So what do you think I should do?"

"Well, my editors wanted to go to the authorities. But of course I'm guessing that's not the route you'd want to take, given this guy's claim."

"Uh, no. No it isn't."

"Look, I can't tell you what to do or what not to do. It's pretty obvious that if you try to pay this guy off, he could screw you and still do something with the evidence he has. Or maybe not. He might just be satisfied that he scored some cash. Five grand isn't a lot to you, but it's a lot to a lot of people. My point is, I'll be happy to share his number with you and everything he's sent us. But beyond that, you're on your own."

"Thanks, Ken. Thanks. Yeah, please get me that stuff asap. Don't text it – just make a paper copy and drop it off here. I'll reimburse you for your time."

"Not necessary, D. Keeping you in business is good for my business. Just promise me I'll be the first call you make if you ever have a scoop I can print."

"The very first call. You're a buddy. I owe ya."

Two days later, Tom got a visit from a very big fella who cornered him outside his house. Nine devastating punches and five violent kicks later, it was clear that Tom was not going to be getting any blackmail money from anyone.

"Ya evah tawk about this again," the very big

fella said in a heavy Brooklyn accent, "I'll come back heres and cut yer fuckin' dick off. Got me, pal?"

Tom had to miss two weeks of school while the injuries quasi-healed. He knew he'd never be able to pass off the stitches, black eyes and arm sling to the other teachers as the product of an innocent fall.

Jerry Proud wasn't so lucky. He had called Jeff Josephs back the next day, as he had promised, using a new burner phone. Josephs told him he'd somehow raised the fifty grand and was ready to have it delivered to a designated drop point of Jerry's choosing.

But Jerry wasn't born yesterday; he knew the drop point might be staked out, and he wasn't going to just walk into a trap. So he sent Leslie.

Yes, that's right – the brilliant criminal mastermind sent his wife to pick up his blackmail money!

When he spotted the swarm of FBI agents closing in on her from the driver's seat of their powder blue VW van parked two blocks away, Jerry peeled out and never looked back. That's when it first dawned on him that his wife would give him up in a heartbeat; she wasn't going to do hard time in prison for his crime. So he didn't go home. He just drove and drove, stopping only once to lift some clean plates off an abandoned motorhome.

When he was about four hundred miles out of Nevada and felt pretty confident he hadn't been followed, he booked a motel room with the cash Ken had paid him and hunkered down in central California to think his way out of this fuckup.

Chapter 9

*O*n the morning of the *Dinnertime University* covenant wedding seminar, everybody seemed upset. Myra was pissed at Derek for re-marrying her. Derek was still pissed at Myra for trying to blackmail him.

Jeff Josephs was mad that he had to drive all the way to Griffith Park on a Saturday to babysit his biggest female client while she made amends for her very screwed up love life.

Jerry was pissed at Jeff Josephs for siccing the FBI on him, causing his wife to be arrested for being an accessory to extortion.

Leslie was furious at her idiot husband Jerry for telling her he had a surprise gift for her and it was just "over there in the park in a briefcase under the red bench," damning her to a possible fifteen year prison term.

Jerry was also pissed at the FBI for screwing up his plans and possibly leaving his kids de facto orphans. (Jerry hadn't checked in on them since Leslie got nabbed and he took off, but he assumed her parents or someone else were taking care of them.) Now he was running from the FBI and running out of cash. $750 doesn't go far when you're living on the lamb.

Lorraine was angry at her famous boyfriend Derek who was ghosting her. (And had indeed gotten her pregnant.)

Tom Reiner was pissed because the Myra and Derek covenant marriage class idea had been stolen from him. And because he got the snot beaten out of him for trying to get back at them.

Ken was pissed because his editors had nixed two amazing hard news stories about the hottest couple in Hollywood, but now wanted him to "cover" this stupid publicity stunt. Here he was, a trained journalist and one-time Pulitzer nominee who had originally broken the story of how covenant marriages were being abused back in the early 2000s, and he had to sit on two major leads about the negative impact of covenants on the lives of real people.

Helen Fay Crittenden was pissed because she was no longer the biggest celebrity in the *Dinnertime University* stable of instructors. And because someone had clearly stolen her life story and was making a TV sitcom pilot about a fictional murderess turned murder tutor that was being developed for Myra Dreyer.

Upon learning about it, Helen went ballistic and was poised to sue. But in an inspired bit of legal genius, Jeff Josephs insisted that the fictional heroine secretly confess to her guilt to a close friend in the pilot episode. Because while Helen had been acquitted of her mariticide, she dared not file a lawsuit claiming a TV series about a *confessed* husband murderer was based on her. If she did that, her lawyers explained, she'd open herself up to lawsuits from her late husband's children and first two wives, all of whom he was supporting when he died. Helen railed to her lawyers about the legal Sword of Damocles hanging over her and vowed revenge.

Lisa Prococino was upset because her call to Jerry Proud to warn him about Ken's call had been traced back to her through his phone records by the FBI, who had also been searching for her in connection with the suspicious death of her rich parents, who had mysteriously died of carbon monoxide poisoning a week after they had each taken out a $3 million life insurance policy with

Lisa as sole beneficiary. Suspicious because 1) they had five children but had only taken out life insurance for their estranged daughter Lisa; 2) the car that was found running in their garage that caused the deadly CO fumes didn't belong to them; it had been stolen the night before while parked in front of the building their daughter lived in; 3) both their bodies had traces of Ativan in their systems, even though neither of them had a prescription for the sleep-inducing drug; 4) their soon-to-be-wealthy daughter Lisa *did* have a prescription for Ativan; 5) Lisa mysteriously fled to the white beaches of Tulum, Mexico soon after her parents' deaths, not waiting to do little things like tell her friends and family that she was moving or to attend her parents' funerals.

Upon finding her number connected to Jerry's phone line, the FBI placed a call to her from Jerry's number (spoofing his digits) and she picked up, allowing them to trace her to her condo in Tulum. Now she was being held by the Mexican authorities while the United States frantically tried to extradite her from one of the few nations in the civilized word that won't extradite a murder suspect back to a capital offense country. An extradition effort made difficult due to the extremely harsh new death penalty laws that had been instated following the Trey Pruitt Scott Supreme Court case that had made a first-degree murder sentence of death by hitman a legal throughout the fifty states.

Oh, and Mrs. Yoeste was upset because English teacher-slash-opera lover Dominick Brody turned out to be gay.

So, as thousands of star-struck movie fans and religious fanatics converged on Griffith Park to see Myra and Derek talk about their magical covenant marriage, these various seeds of anger were taking root and blossoming into the warm Los Angeles morning air.

Tom had his free ticket and was trying to put some coverup makeup over his facial wounds that had yet to fully heal. Indeed, Tom had been so spooked by the violent attack that he went out and bought a handgun for self-protection. And he would be carrying it with him in his pocket today. *Just in case someone tries to fuck with me there,* Tom rationalized to himself. *Or maybe – just maybe – I can pull it to make a point with those two movie star pervs.* Tom fantasized about seeing Derek and Myra squirm and beg for their lives starring down the barrel of his new Glock 43. Wouldn't it be great, he dreamed, of seeing those two super-rich, super-spoiled sexual degenerates beg him for their lives in front of a crowd of thousands?! *Yes,* Tom reveled in thought, *maybe I'll just teach them the kind of life lesson you can't learn in a Dinnertime University classroom.*

Ken had his press credentials and was hoping to get an interview with the mega-star couple before the event, hopefully as a payback favor from Derek.

Lorraine took $195 dollars out of the mysterious college fund that had somehow been created for her and bought a ticket and a pretty new red sheer blouse in the hopes of using her wicked figure to catch the eye of her dreamy ex-boyfriend.

Jerry Proud had driven back to L.A. after attaching huge mobile billboards to each side of his powder blue VW van. The billboards were emblazoned with the words, *"Say 'I Do' to Covenant Marriages"* in giant lettering with roses and red hearts painted all around. But Jerry wasn't on his way to Griffith Park to promote non-divorceable marriage. He was going there because *his* covenant marriage had brought so much grief and torment to his miserable life that he wanted to spread that same misery to as many people as humanly possible.

Super-agent Jeff Josephs had a free ticket

because he gets a free ticket to everything. His former desk person, Adrian, had a free ticket that he stole off Jeff's desk the day Jeff fired him. And the mailroom kid who takes Jeff's car to be detailed had a free ticket because he had just been promoted to be Jeff's new desk person.

Helen Fay Crittenden had a free ticket because all *Dinnertime University* instructors had been invited to the promotional event to hawk their own courses. But Helen being Helen, had to take things one step further by setting up a book signing table and handing out souvenir Helen Fay Crittenden signature claw hammers with their blood-red hammer head. "One for each happily married couple," her booth signage said. The joke was not lost on the people who grabbed them up.

The only people who weren't there yet were Derek and Myra, who would be found dead hours later in his Pacific Palisades home – the victims of an apparent murder-suicide. Also discovered at the gruesome crime scene was the body of their live-in chef, Anastasia, a rather gorgeous 20-year old student chef who had recently arrived from Greece and had gotten a little too close to her famous, hunky boss for Myra's taste. Derek and Anastasia's bodies were found bloody and naked in her upstairs bedroom, stabbed some 118 times between them.

Myra was found in the massive backyard, laying calmly under the stars, a glass of Pinot in one hand and an antique Colt .45 in the other, a single bullet hole in her temple.

◆ ◆ ◆ ◆ ◆

The crowd was estimated at 5,000 people half an hour before the much heralded "Covenant Kingdom" seminar was scheduled to start, with an estimated 3,000 more turned away at the ticket booths. It was so sprawling it had to be festival seating, with people camped on blankets and under canopy tents waiting for "class" to begin.

Toward the back, Tom Reiner was fuming with anger. This was HIS idea. HIS booking. HIS vision. Stolen from him, like every other good thing that never happened in his miserable little life! *How did this all go so far astray? All I ever wanted to do was bring some morality and decency into the world. But this, this is a circus. A mockery of holy matrimony. A mockery of ME!*

With his hand firmly on handle of the Glock in his pocket, Tom began to weave through the maze of blankets and canopies trying to get closer to the stage. *In case they announce my course,* Tom rationalized. *Or in case the don't!* Now madder than he'd ever felt, Tom strode purposefully through the crowd toward the empty chairs that would soon be occupied by the two *happy, sexy, rich jerks* who had stolen his idea and his self-worth.

Just then, a familiar voice stopped him.

"No, I'm telling you, Charlotte. Right side, forth row from the back. I'm in a bright red, see-though blouse."

"Lorraine?" Tom called out loud enough from a distance of fifteen feet to be heard over the noisy crowd.

Lorraine Leaver turned around to spot him – "Mr. Reiner?" – and suddenly struck the most terrifying expression Tom had ever seen on a human face. *Wow, am I really that unpopular with my students?*

"Look out!" she screamed.

Tom Reiner spun around to see what was to be the last miserable image of his miserable life: a pale blue VW van, with billboards boasting the words *Say 'I do' to Covenant Marriage* on each side, speeding right at him.

Like a raging bull in a bullring, Jerry saw something bright red in front of him and raced right toward it. The ensuing carnage spread down a path almost two hundred feet long. Bodies flew through the sky while others were crushed under the VW's almost bald tires. Several were dragged to their deaths before the car came to a rest under the makeshift raised stage that had been decorated as a wedding alter.

The final statistics were horrifying. One hundred four people killed, 218 hospitalized, fourteen of them requiring amputations. It was the worst single vehicle car death toll in American history. Among the victims CNN eulogized on screen were a highly-respected high school guidance counselor and one of his 16-year old female students. Also caught in the carnage was a Galaxy Talent agent, his former assistant, and the young man who had just replaced him. Just grim coincidences of the worst case of vehicular terrorism in modern history.

The driver, who was pulled from the car and beaten pretty badly before being subdued by police, was one Gerald Jackson ("Jerry") Proud, a cybersecurity software salesman who claimed he had lost control of the vehicle trying to avoid running into a police horse, and in a moment of panic mistakenly hit the gas pedal instead of the brake. A police horse had been the first victim of the deadly tragedy, so his story seemed plausible at first.

But as reporters began to dig into his background, more and more tidbits came out that seemed to put dents in his alibi. For instance, an *American Peephole* reporter named Ken Feldman wrote that he had met Mr. Proud at an adult education class about how to get away with murder. Ironically, the class was sponsored by *Dinnertime University*, the same people who had sponsored the "Covenant Kingdom" event.

More digging led to a tip from the course instructor and an amputee victim of the tragedy, Helen Fay Crittenden, who turned over to police an essay one of one of her students had turned in for her final exam titled, "Gas Pedal or Brake: Five Surefire Ways to Infuse Reasonable Doubt in Your Spouse's Demise." The paper had been written by a thirty year-old woman named Lisa Prococino, a classmate of Proud's, who was now a fugitive in Mexico. But the police had reports that the two may have known each other intimately, and speculated they could have planned the attack together since Proud's alibi so closely mirrored Prococino's "Reasonable Doubt" essay.

That story was published by *The American Peephole* under the headline, "Killer Teaches Killers: the bloody bloodline from Helen to Lisa to Jerry to Myra" with photos of the grisly Chase-Dreyer crime scene decorating the cover. The byline on the article belonged to Ken Feldman.

In the nineteen years following the Covenant Murders, as they came to be known, the legal system sputtered and coughed along as Jerry Proud was tried, convicted of 84 first degree murders, and sentenced to death. (Actually, twenty-six death sentences, making him the death row inmate with the most death sentence convictions in San Quintin or any other U.S. prison, for that matter.) And his appeals were still going. The only reason he had not been put to death already for his capital murder convictions was that he was able to use the Trey Pruitt Scott defense that two of his victims, Tom Reiner and Lorraine Leaver, had seen his VW van barreling at them and "knew" they were going to die before it happened. So giving him the electric chair would be too similarly cruel and unusual, according to that landmark 6-3 Supreme Court decision.

During those nineteen years, covenant marriages became more and more popular throughout the United States. Sometimes called "Myra Marriages," they were meant to deter so-called no-fault divorces, whose root causes, it was believed, were philandering and domestic abuse. The logic being, if couples knew they had to stay together no matter what, maybe they would honor their wedding vows from the get-go.

Meanwhile, rightwing legislatures continued to tighten the grip of covenant marriages, and in at least nine states, there were no legal grounds whatsoever for a covenant marriage spouse to file for divorce. You were simply chained to your no-good, cheating, abusive husband or wife for the rest of your living years. Or theirs. Which meant that Covenant Murders (aka "Derek Divorces") were on the rise as well.

By Ken's estimates – he was researching it for a book on covenants – there had been over twelve thousand suspicious deaths or outright murders in the United States that involved one or both spouses in a covenant marriage. Dozens of them involved "peddle confusion" automobile accidents. Scores more involved suspicious carbon monoxide poisonings. And at least fourteen involved unexplainable hammer claw wounds.

But there were also beautiful, happy, lasting marriages. Young marriages that blossomed over time. Established marriages with renewed vows that brought even deeper meaning to a lifetime of commitment. There was even a rumored covenant polyamorous marriage between a man, his wife, and her much younger male lover. However, the laws on polyamory marriage were far behind the times of same-sex marriage, with only two states, Oregon and Hawaii, recognizing them. And it certainly was not ordained by the Catholic Church. Sadly, love was still defined by law and tradition more than by human feelings.

It wasn't the covenants that were good or bad, Ken came to realize. Like anything invented by humans, from the atom bomb to a miracle pain killer, it isn't the invention that's bad. It's how you use or abuse it.

The Supreme Court had changed its make-up during that time as well. Whizz Honor had passed away at the ripe old age of 91. And Justice of the Piece had died of a gunshot wound through the eyeball while he was cleaning his antique Colt .45. (The same model he had gifted Myra and Derek for their wedding.) So there was hope that a new, more liberal court, might strike down both covenant marriage laws and the death penalty. But as test cases made their ways through the state and federal courts, thousands more lives were being torn asunder by bad laws passed with good intentions.

Of course, all that meant nothing to Jerry Proud. He was still doing time in San Quentin, his children had long ago disavowed him, his ex-wife never visited (*"Bitch!"* he thought). And his lawyers were hoping to use his case to challenge the death penalty once and for all in this country. Jerry's case had garnered tons of media coverage because of his story: a working stiff and dedicated father trapped in a loveless covenant marriage and broken down by the very religious orthodoxy he was promoting on his van the day of the crash.

Jerry continued to claim that the rampage was indeed an accident and not premeditated murder. And quite a large segment of America bought his story, even if the police and twenty-six juries didn't.

On the morning of Sunday, September 1, Jerry was told by a guard that he had an 11:00 a.m. appointment in the visitors' room with his lawyer, Robert F. Lowenstein, the same defense attorney who had helped Trey Pruitt Scott get his death sentence overturned three decades earlier. Jerry only wanted the best on his case.

Jerry combed his hair, put on a fresh orange jumpsuit, and appeared at the appointed time for the escort to the visitor's room. Jerry had just polished off a large breakfast of steak and lobster, the result of an unusual act of kindness by his guards, who for some strange reason asked Jerry that morning if he'd like anything special for breakfast.

"Anything you want, Proud. Just name it."

Jerry joked "Steak and lobster," and to his incredulity, the gourmet meal appeared at ten a.m. sharp. *Hmm, guess I must have some fans around here,"* Jerry mused to himself as he gorged on the first decent meal he'd had in nineteen years.

At 10:58 Jerry was escorted into the visitors' room, which he thought was unusually empty for a Sunday morning. By exactly 11:00 Jerry was seated in the visitor area, but his attorney seemed to be running late. At a table near Jerry was a new inmate, a very big fella named Sal who had a heavy Brooklyn accent and was rumored to be a mafia enforcer of some kind. Suddenly, the lights in the room blinked twice. *"Was the power going out?"* Jerry wondered. *"Hey, wouldn't it be funny if it was because they were stealing current to electrocute some inmate?"*

As Jerry started to smile at his own joke, Sal stood up, pulled out a nine millimeter Beretta, and pumped four bullets into Jerry Proud's left temple. Jerry slumped face-down on the table.

Sal handed the Beretta to one of the guards, then shook his hand and walked out the back door of the room, passing a woman visitor in a yellow flowered dress as she held hands with a man in a business suit and sunglasses.

"Mr. and Mrs. Leaver," the warden addressed the couple softly, indicating toward the doorway.

After a moment of reflection, holding back tears, Lorraine Leaver's parents stood up, nodded to the warden, and solemnly left the room.

The End

ACKNOWLEDGEMENTS

I want to thank Doug McIntyre, Jean McCormick, Mark Rappaport, and Jessica Wallraff for their input and editorial guidance on this book.

About the Author

Kevin Kelton is an Emmy-nominated writer with credits on *Saturday Night Live, Night Court, Boy Meets World, National Lampoon* and TV specials for Jay Leno and Steve Martin. Super Vows is his first venture into long-form fiction. His second novel, Pas De Deux, will be published in 2022.

Made in the USA
Middletown, DE
14 January 2022